The Curse of the Seer

Legends of Tira-Nor
Book Three

Daniel Schwabauer

Legends of Tira-Nor: The Curse of the Seer
Book three in the Legends of Tira-Nor series

Copyright © 2015 by Daniel Schwabauer

Published by Living Ink Books, an imprint of
AMG Publishers, Inc.
6815 Shallowford Rd.
Chattanooga, Tennessee 37421

All rights reserved. Except for brief quotations in printed reviews, no part of this publication may be reproduced, stored in a retrieval system, or transmitted in any form or by any means (printed, written, photocopied, visual electronic, audio, or otherwise) without the prior permission of the publisher.

This is a work of fiction. Names, characters, places, and incidents either are the product of the author's imagination or are used fictitiously. Any resemblance to actual persons, either living or dead, events, or locales is entirely coincidental.

First Printing—July 2015

Print edition	ISBN 13: 978-0-89957-850-7
EPUB edition	ISBN 13: 978-1-61715-373-0
Mobi edition	ISBN 13: 978-1-61715-374-7
ePDF edition	ISBN 13: 978-1-61715-375-4

THE LEGENDS OF TIRA NOR® is a trademark
of AMG Publishers

Cover layout and design by Carrol Schwabauer

Editing by Christy Graeber and Rick Steele

Interior design and typesetting by
Adept Content Solutions LLC, Urbana, IL

Printed in the United States of America
20 19 18 17 16 15 -V- 6 5 4 3 2 1

To the Garner family:

*Laird, Amy, Rachel, Grace, Carolyn, Isaiah,
Michal Anne, Penny, Adelle and Eleanor.*

*For remaining with us
though you moved away.*

Contents

Pronunciation Guide

AaNoth: an oth
AlBaer: al bear
Cadrid: cad rid
DeVree: da vree
ElShua: el shoo uh
Glyn: glin
Hammah: ha ma
IsaBel: is a bell
Kalla: call a
KoTsu: coat soo
LiDel: lid el
PaTri: pa tree
RuHoff: roo hoff
SimHone: sim own
Tira-Nor: tier uh nor
TuRue: too roo

the
Royal
Palace
Royal
West
the
Kingsguard
The
Families
The
Great
Hall
Open
Common
Shade
Wind

TIRANOR
the Tunnels
North
Mud
Seed
Tower
East (gate)
The Commons
N
T
Forest
denotes a gate

RuHo
Cav
Tall Grass
Tira-N
Dry Gully
Round Top
The Da
Forest
To West
Exiter
White River
TyMin's Path

North Meadows
The Wall
Pond
Cabin
Bridge
To The Deep
Unknown
KNOWN WORLD
N
W
E
S
g's
ry

Chapter One

The Audience

I saw the shadow enter the king's head. Black-bodied and long as a weasel, it slid into his open mouth from the darkness of the far wall. It was only a flicker of movement in the corner of my eye; it might have been a shadow cast, perhaps, from a dying glowstone. But I knew better, even with my head bowed and my gaze shifting from the close-packed dirt floor to the royal dais.

The king pursed his lips before speaking. "It is a fair offer, LiDel," he said.

Queen IsaBel nodded. Her tail twitched like a cat's. She smiled at me, her face as colorless as ice.

I stood exactly nine paces from the dais. Father stood next to me, his right forepaw still gripping my neck, a warning not to speak.

King Ahaz and Queen IsaBel were like blood and pus. He was the wound, she the infection.

"It is more than fair," the queen added. "For such a small chamber. In the *Commons*." She enunciated the last word.

"We shall grant you larger quarters near the Seed Gate. Something more . . ." Ahaz waved one paw, ". . . more suitable for one of your station. A widower, not so young, with a growing boy to feed. Think of your future."

The Seed Gate. How generous!

Father tightened his grip on the fur of my neck. He must have sensed the sarcastic remark I was polishing. "It is not that your price is too low, Majesties. It is that, as you say, I must think of my future." He motioned to me with his free left forepaw. "Our home has been passed down from father to kit for fifteen generations. It is neither a large nor an elegant home. But it is ours. It bears our name, our history. I could not—"

"LiDel," Queen IsaBel interrupted. "Do you really think we don't have your son's best interests in mind?" She stared at him unblinking, her face expressionless and terrifying.

Father looked from the queen to me. "I have no doubt about that," he said, his voice soft.

"So you will sell?" King Ahaz leaned forward, his great froglike eyes eager.

"My Lord," Father said, "what would that teach the boy? That anything and everything is for sale? That there is nothing a simple mouse can own that can't be bought?"

The queen's eyes narrowed. Her lips drew together in a frown—perhaps from gravity, perhaps by force of habit.

"No, Majesties," Father continued. "Our home was granted to us in ancient times by TyMin himself, as an everlasting reward for—"

"Surely," King Ahaz said, stepping off the dais, "you don't believe a simple tradition is more important than the goodwill of your king?"

Father relaxed his grip, and I saw my chance. I pulled myself free and looked up, wishing I had the legendary strength of Glyn the Strong, or at the very least his fabled wit in the presence of his enemies. "How can confiscating our home be called goodwill?"

"Eli!" Father regained his hold on my neck and squeezed. I yelped, more from spite than actual pain. "I told you to hold your tongue."

"But—"

"Hold your tongue!"

King Ahaz watched the exchange without moving, his lips pouting above double chins that shook with displeasure.

"I apologize for my son's rudeness, Your Highness."

"Your son, yes. He is another matter. I am told he was caught trespassing in the temple of Kalla. He is responsible for much damage."

"It's a lie," I blurted. "I didn't—"

Father squeezed. He bent forward and pulled my head up. His eyes flashed a warning. I'd never seen him so angry.

"A lie?" The queen asked in a high, mocking voice. "A lie?"

Father closed his eyes for a moment, then straightened his back and looked Her Majesty full in the face. "What my foolish and outspoken son, who is terrible with words, meant to say, Your Highness, is not that you are in any way wrong, but that the reports you have heard of his responsibility in the matter of the damaged herbs have been exaggerated."

She squeezed out a brief, ugly laugh like a hiccup. "I see your son who is terrible with words does not take after you. But exaggerated or not, he has admitted he was in the temple of Kalla without permission. I should like to hear him speak for himself." Her face belied her words, and I knew it was a challenge. She meant for me to say something stupid to be used against us.

Something else stupid.

Father gave me another look of warning and let go of my neck.

"Your Highness," I said, facing the king.

"Were you in the temple of Kalla?"

"Yes. I was chased there by—"

"Without permission?" The king stepped closer and glared down at me. He was a tall mouse, who, if rumors are to be believed, once carried a good deal of muscle on his now fat frame.

I took a deep breath. "I was chased there by two acolytes who—"

"And *while* you were in the temple of Kalla without permission you managed to befoul a month's supply of . . ." He turned to the queen for help.

"Maywort," she said.

"A month's supply of maywort!" He turned back to me, and it seemed I was looking, not into the king's eyes, but into those of a cold, black weasel.

I shuddered and looked down.

"Majesty," I said, speaking rapidly. "I will not deny stepping in a small cache of leaves that might have been maywort—though more likely it was dried honeysuckle—but I didn't befoul anything." I risked a glance up. "Except my father's reputation."

"Reputation?" Ahaz sneered. "Yes. Well. PaTri says the damage was extensive. And of much more value than a simple mouse's reputation. A month's supply of maywort! A month's supply . . . for the temple. More than any mouse of the Commons could possibly afford to pay back in a lifetime." He stared at Father. "How will you manage?"

Father's face went pale. "I don't know," he said.

Queen IsaBel rose and stepped forward, her steps as light and airy as the king's were ponderous. "There is of course a reasonable alternative. We would be willing to make restitution to PaTri for the maywort if you accept our offer."

Father glanced down at me and I could almost see his mind turning over. "You are most gracious, Majesties," he said. "After fifteen generations . . . may I have a few days to consider your . . . generosity?"

Ahaz stared at him for a long moment. "PaTri has asked that the boy be punished."

"I will thrash him myself," Father said. This surprised me. He had never thrashed me. Never needed to thrash me. His displeasure had always been punishment enough.

"That was not what he had in mind."

"Then we are both grateful," Father said, bowing low, "that Ahaz, and not PaTri, is our king."

Queen IsaBel sighed and looked away. "We shall hear from you tomorrow," she said.

Chapter Two

AlBaer

The palace guards ushered us through the kingsguard section of Tira-Nor and left us in the evening bustle of the Great Hall. They said nothing. Just slipped back into the calm order of the palace.

I took a step forward through the Great Hall, intending to make for what was still, temporarily, our home.

Father put one hand on my shoulder. "Wait," he said.

At the south end of the Great Hall, scavenger slaves, returning from their afternoon shifts, staggered down the ramp from the Common Gate, their mouths stuffed with spring: white roots and fresh berries, clover, honeysuckle, and dandelion.

Longer days meant more time to fill the storage chambers of the city, for King Ahaz didn't know the meaning of enough. More work, more sweat, more slaves bought and sold between Tira-Nor and its newest trade partner, Cadrid.

Father didn't want to walk through the approaching mice, though not because it would take more energy to press past them. It wasn't that he despised them, either. Father remained one of the few Tira-Norans I knew who was capable of true compassion for a stranger. "I am him, and he is me," he sometimes said. And yet, though he pitied them, he also knew that desperation often sired stupidity. Better to wait and let them pass.

These slaves, according to the record of the court, were either criminals or debtors. All of them hailed from other lands. Tira-Nor's unfortunates were sent to Cadrid, where, as Father pointed out, they would have no friends to help them escape.

Midway up the ramp, just visible above the flow of incoming bodies, stood the evening taskmaster, a huge brute of a mouse with a cruel face. He snarled and kicked out at the last mouse to stumble wearily down the ramp.

Father grimaced. After my outburst in the palace, I was too ashamed to urge him on, but neither did I want to take the long way 'round through one of the eastern tunnels. We waited.

"I promised to thrash you," Father said.

I gave him a quizzical look.

"Paws to the wall," he said.

The last of the slaves shuffled past, their faces beaten down.

I turned slowly and pressed my palms against the smooth mud plaster. I clenched my teeth, expecting pain, but felt only three light taps across my back. His tail might have been thumping at flies.

"Consider yourself thrashed," Father said.

I turned and looked at him.

He shrugged. "They may ask about it tomorrow. If they do, tell the truth. I thrashed you in the Great Hall. Always tell the truth, Eli. Understand me?" He cocked his head to one side. "What's wrong?"

"We're going to give them our chamber."

He touched my shoulder and led me south through the Great Hall, toward the tunnel that would lead us home. He spoke softly. "Is that what you think we should do?"

"I don't see what choice we have." Because our quarters were one of the ancient places of Tira-Nor handed down by TyMin himself, the king couldn't legally take them. But a king's power is really only limited by his imagination—never by law.

"We have the choice of free mice," Father said. "We can be bullied and comfortable, or we can be fools and free—and very uncomfortable."

"Won't he just find a way to take it from us?"

"Probably."

"Will we fight him?"

He chuckled. "No, son. We could not win that fight."

"Then what do you mean? How can we say no if the king will just take it from us?"

"It isn't complicated, Eli. I will say no as tactfully as I can, and the king will order us to pay Lord PaTri his extortion money, which we do not have, and then, most likely, I will be sold to Cadrid. Though I expect the going rate for a mouse of my age is nowhere near enough to—"

"Father, you can't!" I grabbed his shoulders and looked into his face. The fur above his eyes lay salted with gray against his forehead, a detail I had never noticed. When had he aged? "It's not your fault!"

And, I thought, what would happen to me?

"Oh, son," he said. "You mustn't feel responsible."

I didn't just feel responsible. I was responsible. "If I hadn't gone into the temple—"

"If. But you had no choice. What else could you have done?"

"I could have fought them. Like Glyn—"

"Life isn't like that, son. Glyn's strength would not have helped you. Besides, you told me you weren't running from the acolytes as much as from —."

It was true. Mitts and Spew—not their real names—were bigger than me, and on my best day I couldn't have beaten both of them. But they were not why I ran.

"But what good will it do for you to be sold and sent away?"

"Good? No good at all that I can see. But the alternative—"

"It's just a chamber!" I shouted.

He pressed one finger to my lips. "It isn't just a chamber. It's a principle. Tyrants must be resisted. When we stop saying no, they will stop feeling the need to ask. And then there will be no free mice left in Tira-Nor. The Commons will be enslaved."

We started walking again. I spoke slowly, trying to control my frustration. "That's a great philosophy, but this is real. Let someone else resist them."

"Everyone in the city is letting someone else resist them. That is the problem. If Tira-Nor is to be free, someone must do something. It always comes down to someone somewhere. It always comes down to one mouse."

Father stopped in the tunnel. When I looked back he motioned for me to follow him down a dark, narrow passage that led due east.

"Where are we going?"

"Down."

"Why?"

"You have a kind of gift, Eli. Perhaps if we lived in a different time, that gift would be appreciated."

Appreciated? I thought. *Even I don't appreciate it.* "So what's down here? It's pretty dark."

He didn't answer. He plodded down a winding ramp, and the air grew colder. We reached the lowest level of the eastern section of the city, where the tunnels were narrow and rarely traveled, and the new quarters, scraped out of the clay, were badly lit.

"*Really* dark down here," I said. My voice rose, and I told myself to just shut up. Father had always said he understood, but how could he? Darkness didn't bother him. He didn't see the dark ghosting shapes, the raspberry eyes, the transparent tails that disappeared into walls. He only knew the darkness bothered me. He wouldn't take me somewhere that gave me the jitters without a reason. That thought made me shiver even more.

Near a fading glowstone he paused long enough to smile at me. We stood alone in the corridor outside a poor chamber from which greenish light spilled. He scratched at the entrance.

"Not done yet," a cheerful voice called from inside. "Seventeen. Eighteen. Nineteen. TWENTY!"

A long, thin face appeared in the entrance, smiling above two wiry paws.

It was the ancient lunatic, AlBaer. I took a step back.

AlBaer's smile widened. "Not expecting you," he said. "Busy now. Come again later." He disappeared.

Silence.

Father waited a moment before scratching the entrance again.

"Still busy!" AlBaer's voice echoed from the chamber. "Come again later."

Father pursed his lips. "It is important, Master AlBaer."

A long pause, followed by: "Yes, yes, important. Very important, no doubt. But we are busy now. Come again later."

"Shall we wait?" Father asked.

Another long pause. AlBaer's nose appeared again in the doorway. "Yes?"

"Shall we wait?"

"Wait no longer. The king is very angry with AlBaer. You would do well to avoid my company."

"Angry? Why?"

AlBaer looked at me for a long moment, then back at Father. "He has discovered the reason for the drought. He knows I asked ElShua. No rain. No dew. Not so much as a long spit in the dust. A curse spoken by the king's own seer. A curse he does not appreciate.

The king blames the drought on me." He smiled. "And he is right."

"The king is angry with us too."

"Yes?"

"Yes."

AlBaer fingered his chin. "Your quarters, I suspect."

I shot Father a surprised glance.

"In fact, yes," Father said.

"The king!" AlBaer shook his head and frowned for the first time. "The king—is a twit. Tell him that for me."

He disappeared inside.

Father stared at the chamber hole. After a moment he called into it: "Master AlBaer, we need your help."

"Busy now. Come again later."

Father sighed. "My son, Eli. He sees things, Master AlBaer. I thought perhaps you might take him in as an apprentice."

"Apprentice!" I said. "But Father—"

AlBaer's face appeared again. He bit into a slice of browning apple and chewed thoughtfully. "I don't need an apprentice. Only slow me down."

"Where are you going?"

"Away."

"My son has a gift."

"Everyone has a gift. If only I had a gift for every time a proud parent—"

"I'm not just another proud parent," Father interrupted, his voice soft. "He has a real gift."

"Yes, yes." AlBaer looked at me. "But your son, Eli, can't see. One must see in order to be a seer's apprentice. And in order to see, one must understand the curse of the seer."

Droughts. Apprenticeships. Seers. I kept my mouth shut the length of the conversation more from confusion than good manners. At last I interrupted. "Father, why are we still here?" I asked. "I don't want to be apprenticed to this crazy old windbag. I'd rather be sold to the Cadridians."

"Eli!"

"Old?" AlBaer took a bite of his apple. "Am I old?"

"Master AlBaer—" Father began.

AlBaer chewed expressionlessly, his eyebrows raised.

Father stared at him as the pause stretched into an awkward silence. At last Father said, "Thank you for your time." He looked at me and motioned with his eyes that it was time to leave.

I turned in the corridor and searched the shadows for the ramp up. We started walking.

From behind us, AlBaer called cheerfully, his words muffled by a mouthful of apple, "Don't be afraid, Master LiDel. ElShua is about to promote you."

AlBaer, a seer? Not a chance. The seers in the old stories were mystical and powerful and clever. They spoke in riddles, not nonsense. They used words like *forsooth* and *behold*! They didn't say, "Come again later." The seers of old didn't have arms like twigs and necks no wider than a blade of grass.

Real seers weren't insane.

Chapter Three

Home

They were waiting for us at our ancestral chamber. We never even made it inside for a last look.

Kingsguard mice stepped from the shadows. One of them clubbed Father in the temple, knocking him to the ground.

No one touched me. They didn't need to. My body sprouted roots as two mice hauled Father up and shoved him against the tunnel wall. Oh, I meant to move. In my imagination I leapt forward with arms raised and bashed the heads of the kingsguard warriors against the rounded earthen walls.

In reality, I did nothing. My legs stayed put; my arms hung motionless at my sides. I watched with a feeling of unreality as the chance I had been waiting for unfolded like a slow nightmare, as if everything were happening underwater: the burly kingsguard warriors, the shadows of mice wavering against the walls, Father's left eye squeezed shut against a thick line of blood dribbling around it.

One shadow raised its fist.

I continued to stare. Glyn the Strong wouldn't have just stared. He would have done something. But me? I watched as the fist descended and Father's head snapped sideways. That I did nothing shames me, but it is the truth, and I made a promise to Father that I would always tell the truth. So I will tell the truth now, and not just the good parts—the parts that make me look better than I am. A story recounting my heroism and acts of good character would be short indeed. I could write such a story on the husk of a single grain of wheat.

But my shame is greater still, for I didn't just do nothing. I expected Father to fight back. I expected him to struggle, to lash out with fists or tail, to at least resist them.

He did not resist. He took their blows, and when he coughed up a long trail of bloody spittle, I grew angry with him! He should have done something! He should have fought them. He should have tried! And even if he had failed, well . . .

Glyn the Strong would have fought them.

"What do you say to the king's offer now, LiDel?" one of the kingsguard warriors asked. His voice came with no anger, no sympathy, no expectations of any kind.

Father looked at me, his face a mess, and even through all the blood and swelling I recognized a deep sadness. I knew the expression. He wanted to tell me he was sorry. He wanted to tell me that he wished there were some other way. But someone had to stand up to the king. Someone had to pay the price of opposing Ahaz, and if not him, who?

"The king . . ." Father said, looking up at the officer, ". . . is a tyrant . . . and a twit. Tell him . . ."

He never finished the sentence.

The kingsguard mouse jabbed Father in the throat with the fingers of his left paw, a short movement like flicking away a gnat.

Father's eyes bulged. He looked at me and gagged out a strangled, throaty command, no louder than a whisper: "Run!"

Still I stood there, wanting to go to him, wanting—ElShua help me—to leave him, but unable to move.

"Father!"

One of the kingsguard brutes plucked me from the earth with a meaty arm and held me in front of his whiskerless face. I kicked out at him, screaming, until he clamped a paw over my mouth.

I tried to bite the paw, but the grip was too tight. I could barely breathe.

The mice holding Father's wrists let go, and he collapsed in a heap, one arm thrust awkwardly out, his eyes open.

I wanted to scream again, but no sounds would come. My heart had frozen into a solid chunk of ice the moment I looked into Father's eyes and knew he wasn't looking back.

"Take the boy to the pens," the officer commanded. "He won't bring much. But then, I doubt PaTri really lost a month's supply of maywort." The others chuckled. The guard carrying me changed his grip as he started down the tunnel.

I yanked my right paw free and bashed him in the eye.

He swore and then hit me back so hard I thought I would pass out. Instead, I vomited across his back. A second—albeit tiny and miserable—moment of revenge that did not satisfy my rage.

I hated them with a great, monstrous fury that spread through my veins like liquid fire. I hated the mouse carrying me. I hated the other soldiers, the ones who murdered Father. I hated the officer; the mice of the kingsguard; the stupid, fat, and silent mice of Tira-Nor who watched and listened from their chamber holes but did nothing—the ones who wouldn't say no to the king regardless of Father's example. I hated King Ahaz and Queen IsaBel.

My captor tied all four of my paws together and threw me onto the straw floor of a storage chamber with a dozen other mice bound for Cadrid. I saw that his eye had started to blacken, but the little black lump wasn't enough. Not nearly enough. So I cursed him and all the rest of them: the kingsguard, the mice of the city, the king and queen.

Black-Eye just laughed and retreated through the chamber hole.

The others in the room stared at me in silence, so I cursed them too. For good measure I cursed AlBaer and TyMin and Kalla and PaTri and all of Cadrid. I cursed anyone foolish enough to sell or buy me at the slave market. I would not work, no matter what they did to me. Only when my throat throbbed with a raw burning did I stop raging curses at my enemies.

A thin blade of light streamed from a hole in the roof. We lay near the surface, near the field that marked the capitol of the Known Lands. The room would be dark as soon as the sun went down.

I thought of Father's last moments: his head snapping sideways, his eyes bulging, his voice like an open wound commanding me to run, while I stood there stupidly and did nothing.

I turned my head to the wall and let the tears come. I had saved my most bitter curse for the last. In the failing light of day I ground my teeth together and silently cursed myself.

Chapter Four

The Auction

Standing behind us on the dirt platform, the taskmaster shoved, prodded, and beat all seventeen of us into a single line. Stewards from the houses of Cadridian nobility paced the floor of the Great Hall with narrowed eyes, apparently looking for signs of weakness or disease. We still reeked of the storage chambers; a mixture of herbs, unwashed bodies, and blood.

I glared at a mouse with black fur who licked at the single rotting tooth that jutted from his ancient gums. He caught my gaze and flashed a humorless smile.

His expression told me he recognized my attitude and would enjoy crushing it.

Except for a couple of rough moments, the task-master had ignored me, pouring out the emotionless venom of his fists on the others in the line, all adults. I doubt he cared about my youth. More likely he just didn't see me as a threat. He never even searched me, which turned out to be bad for both of us. I had found something useful in the straw-matted floor of the storage chamber where we slept, and tucked it into the fur under my left armpit.

PaTri arrived with Mitts and Spew. The acolytes pointed at me and laughed. Mitts cupped his paws to his cheeks and mouthed "maywort" with an exaggerated bob of his thick head. I pretended not to notice.

PaTri, a middle-aged mouse with graying wire-brush fur and a sharp ochre-spotted nose, stood a head taller than everyone else in the room. He held a clear view of the auction but paid little attention to those of us in the line. He seemed engrossed in a business transaction with the Cadridians.

The mice from Cadrid took a long time to examine us. No less than a dozen stewards, lesser nobles, and special detail leaders pinched and prodded my body, peeled back my lips to inspect my teeth, and peered skeptically into my eyes and ears before moving on. The feeling was difficult to describe. We were no different than a hive of suspicious-looking insects, or a shipment of corn, or a stack of raisins—something to be bartered for and used up.

Around me, Tira-Noran officials haggled over price, lied about our age and strength, made promises we would never be able to keep.

Here and there I caught snatches of conversation whispered in the breathy accent of the foreigners, and understood finally that they didn't expect me to survive the trip to Cadrid.

One large mouse with a splotch of brown fur draping his shoulders lifted my chin and looked into my eyes with a kindly expression. "What have we heah?" he said. "A young one. Of common stock. Who, I shall think, does not wish to be sold."

I am not for sale, I thought. But I didn't say it because I knew it would bring me no chance for revenge.

Splotch pinched the muscles in my forearms, then stood back and gazed at me with a thoughtful expression. "I shall think he is clear of mind, and should be treated gently. He would make an excellent overseer." He stroked his chin. "Except—"

Mitts and Spew had worked their way forward and were standing right in front of me, behind Splotch's back. "Except he has no mind," Spew said, and then laughed at his own joke.

If I must be sold, I thought, *it should be to someone else, someone I can hate easily.* I planned to kill whoever purchased me.

"How much for the young one?" a mouse with black fur asked.

The taskmaster seemed to sense an imminent sale and appeared out of nowhere. "Twelve," he said.

Splotch gave the taskmaster a look of amused disbelief and looked back at the black mouse, shaking his head. "I shall think you are dreaming," he said, and started to move on.

"Cost me twice that in maywort," PaTri said from the crowd. "And he is healthy. Anyone can see that."

"Bot he has speerit," Splotch said. He turned away and nudged open the mouth of an old gray-hair to look at his teeth. "We do not need speerit."

"His spirit," PaTri offered, stepping between his two acolytes and glaring down at me from above his ponderous nose, "can be easily broken."

Splotch's eyes flicked to mine and then away. A smile whispered at one corner of his mouth. "As you say."

After a pause, PaTri said, "Nine, then."

Splotch continued to ignore both of us. He took the old mouse's head in his paws and turned it sideways to look in one ear. At last he said, with a sigh, "Two, perhaps."

A look of indignation crossed PaTri's face, and he stepped forward onto the dirt platform directly in front of me. He grabbed the fur on the back of my neck and yanked my head up. "He is young. There are many years of hard work left in this growing body. His teeth are good. His hearing is good. He is agile and—"

Behind PaTri, Mitts cupped his paws to his cheeks. "And ugly," he said.

"Shut up!" PaTri snarled, jerking his head around to look at his two acolytes, who suddenly disappeared into the crowd. He was not looking at me, and that was the first of his three mistakes that day. His second mistake was letting go of my neck.

I barely had to shift my weight forward. I grabbed his forearm with both paws and bit down into the scrawny muscle.

PaTri let out a pitiful, girlish shriek and tried to pull his arm away with his left paw.

He failed.

Spew lunged from somewhere and grabbed me by the shoulders, but his efforts were ridiculous—as though he were not really trying to pull me free.

The taskmaster came quickly, calmly, and Spew let go.

The heavily muscled taskmaster tried to pull me off too, and when that didn't work, he began to beat me about the head. It was all I could do to hold on. PaTri's blood surged around my lips, and my teeth sank deeper and scraped bone. I prayed that I might hit an artery.

The taskmaster wrapped one massive arm around my head and with his other paw grabbed the end of my snout. He heaved backward, and PaTri's arm, alas, came free.

PaTri stared down at the twin punctures, which seemed too small for the pain I knew they would cost me. He clutched his injured forearm in his left paw, his face as yellow-white as limestone. Long lines of blood dribbled down his fingers and spattered the front of the platform. Rage contorted his face. "By the rat," he growled, "you will pay for this."

Splotch watched the incident with a grim, knowing expression, then looked away. The mouse with black fur actually smiled, then nodded. The taskmaster, who still held me in a headlock, slammed his fist into the side of my face.

Agony. Pain spiked through my skull.

The taskmaster cast me forward to the dirt at PaTri's feet. My cheek burned white hot with a pain that was almost unendurable. Almost.

But PaTri's feet were there before me, and I knew I might never have another chance, even as I knew they would kill me for it.

I drew my knees to my chest so my right paw would be concealed, then wrapped my fingers around the thorn I had hidden in my armpit.

PaTri stood above me, his face a mask of fury. "You'll pay!" he fumed. "Do you hear me?" His third mistake. He should not have gloated.

I drove the thorn into his lower left paw, felt the satisfying resistance of flesh, and then dirt, as the thorn went all the way through to the packed earthen floor.

PaTri let out a high, terrified squeal.

Splotch shook his head and scowled.

The taskmaster knelt over me. He raised one fist high above his head.

Coward that I am, I closed my eyes.

Chapter Five

Miracle Mouse

The thing to remember about Glyn the Strong is that he wasn't a myth. He was real.

Of course, even real mice sometimes become legends as the stories of their deeds are swollen by time and retelling. But in the process, the reality of their earth-walk, the whole story of their real mistakes and humiliations and accomplishments, is shaved down to something small and fake. Because it must carry a message, it is made short and understandable. The larger part is bitten off until the life of a real mouse who perhaps was once great is made into the life of a great mouse who perhaps was once real.

Other heroes live only in the stories told by the light of a glowstone in the Great Hall. They are legends, with no shadow of history to color them. They had no earthwalk. They wore no real body. Which is why they can do such great deeds in the Hall stories and not complain of hunger or bloodied knuckles. It is why their great lives are unmarred by mistakes and humiliation.

Not so with Glyn the Strong. He was more than a real mouse, more than a legend. Glyn the Strong was both.

He really lived.

◆ ◆ ◆

His mother and father were married in the Lesser Families. They wore their family title proudly. It was, after all, the only wealth they possessed. Glyn's great-grandfather had squandered the family estate and relocated to sparse, cold little quarters just off the Shade Gate. As close to poverty as one could get without suffering the indignity of the Commons.

Such a fall inspired gossip among even the Greater Families. Whereas Glyn's great-grandfather had eaten at the table of RuHoff the Wise and dined with the descendants of TyMin, Lyn actually had to work. He oversaw a small scavenging crew and frequently returned home in the evening as grubby as the mice under his charge. He rubbed elbows with commoners—laborers who dug and scurried, swore and laughed, and spoke in slang, sometimes even forgetting to call him Sir.

Not that Lyn was the sort to remind anyone of his birthright. He was no prig, and if a common mouse occasionally forgot to say "Sir Lyn," it meant that either he hadn't earned the respect of the formality, or his crew thought so highly of him they considered him one of their own.

Glyn's mother, a soft-spoken mouse with bright eyes and a cheerful smile, suffered her own silent indignities. Gredda hailed from a large, noble family, the youngest of twelve kits. To her shame, she was the only one of the twelve without children. Family gatherings were particularly painful. Not because anyone said anything, but because they didn't. It was the patter of tiny paws, the dozens of little hairless tails, the tiny whiskers and dark eyes of children pleading to be lifted into one's lap that undid her.

After one such occasion, Lyn found Gredda weeping in a dusty alcove. "My dear," he said, wrapping her in his arms, "whatever is the matter?" Though of course he knew. And it was fortunate that he did, for her chest heaved with such great sobs she could not speak. After a moment he pressed her head against his shoulder and said, "There, there, my love," and, "shh, shh, shh," and finally, softly, "we must pray for strength."

She only nodded.

Being both wise and poor, Lyn understood that he couldn't afford the luxury of pretense, and so prayed for more than just strength. He prayed also for humility and wisdom—humility to bear his family shame with honor, and wisdom to know what in the world to do.

Several days later the Ghost Badger found Lyn returning from a long day of scavenging. Dusk painted the sky a violent orange. The Badger stood waist-high in the earth of the Dark Forest, but still he towered over Lyn, who fell face-first into the dirt.

Lyn did not look up, and when he spoke it was as though he were mumbling into a well. "Wumpha annahmhee ahstah!"

He meant, of course, What do you want with me, Master? But he was too frightened to speak clearly, and besides, his nose lay smashed into the dirt.

The badger flipped Lyn over onto his back with one claw. "I have come," the Badger said, "in answer to your prayers. What do you want me to do for you?"

Lyn stared up at the massive, terrifying face. It took him a moment to gather his thoughts, and another moment to work up the courage to speak.

He sat up slowly and considered his answer. What did he want? Well, he could have said happiness, for that did sum up the thing he sought. But Lyn was the sort of mouse who could be happy even when miserable. And though he still feared the Badger's claws and teeth, he was not thinking about himself. So he said, "I want Gredda to be happy. I want a miracle."

The badger cupped his chin in one paw. "Happiness is fleeting, Sir Lyn."

Lyn rose and bowed. "Life is fleeting, Master Badger."

The badger blinked. "For that answer," he said, "you shall have your miracle. But first you must learn the answers to three questions. Behold! You have asked for strength. Therefore, What is stronger than a raisin? You have asked for wisdom. What is wiser than a question asked in the dark? You have asked for humility. What is more humble, Sir Lyn, than a lie?"

The badger did not wait for Lyn to answer. He disappeared like fog before a driving wind, leaving behind only starlight and a terrified, excited noblemouse.

◆ ◆ ◆

Afterward, Lyn repeated the questions to Gredda, who took his paws in her own and said, "You will discover the answers. I believe in you."

And so Lyn traveled alone to the cave of RuHoff the Wise and spent a whole month contemplating the questions. When he returned, he stepped through the chamber hole and smiled at Gredda. "My dear, I believe the boy will be a poet. And he must not eat raisins."

Gredda stared at him. She loved raisins, though they could not often afford them. But did he mean what she thought he meant? "Are you sure?" she asked.

"What is stronger than a raisin if not one's will to resist it?"

"Ah," she said. "And wisdom?"

"Nothing is wiser than a question asked in the dark. All questions are asked in the dark. That is where wisdom begins, by asking for what you don't understand."

Now, at last, she smiled and drew a deep breath, as though with great expectation. "Humility?"

"My dear, a lie is never humble. Real humility is found in the truth. I was never humble until I understood how small and un-noble I really am."

Twenty-one days later, Gredda gave birth to a single gray mouse, a boy who looked strikingly like neither of them.

They named him Glyn.

Chapter Six

Doomed

I awoke in darkness.

The pain began before I opened my eyes. It pierced my dream and throbbed in my mind like a second pulse, pounding in my temple and sending slivers of fire up my left leg.

I lay on my side, blinking. Someone had bound my wrists and ankles together, and though I could turn onto my back, I could not rise to walk.

Darkness.

I didn't know where I was, and the pitch-black

nothingness stretched around me in layers like a shroud. Panic rose in my throat.

I thought of Father. Summoned a cold hatred of his killers to extinguish the fear. Darkness? So what? I could see nothing, therefore darkness didn't matter.

The pain in my left rear paw grew more intense. I strained at the cords, thinking they must have cut off my circulation. My fingers brushed against something hard and unnatural on the back of my paw. I barely touched it, but fresh agony surged through my leg.

A thorn. PaTri's payback.

Hopelessness washed over me. *Surely someone will show pity,* I thought. I grunted out a hoarse, "Hello?"

My voice died away unanswered.

I listened for sounds of movement, of breathing, of life of any kind.

One lone heartbeat. My own.

Eventually, I stopped straining. They had tied me masterfully. I could just feel the head of the thorn with the tips of my fingers, but I could not grasp it to pull it out.

I forced myself to take deep breaths and tried to think of something else.

The room smelled familiar. It felt like Tira-Nor, though I couldn't explain why.

I rolled onto my right side and found that I could scoot very gradually using my hips and elbows. Eventually, I would hit a wall, and then I would at least have something at my back. Given enough time, perhaps I could follow the wall to a chamber hole.

I had not gone far when the first shape slithered into the blackness of the chamber. It slipped through the wall headfirst. Its legs ended in webbed feet splayed out like oak leaves; its tail was as long as a serpent's. Its wide fish's mouth showed no teeth, but shimmered with an ethereal light.

The face curled like fog in the gloom, staring with a lifeless expression. When it spoke, its voice was hard and cold and smooth, like a rock taken from the White River. "Soon," it said, "You will be mine."

I shuddered, but could not take my eyes off its green cartilage lips.

"Soon," it said again.

Light stabbed the darkness, and the creature disappeared. I saw immediately that I lay in a storage chamber piled with stacks of dried herbs. This chamber was smaller than the one that had housed the slaves before the auction.

Someone entered behind me carrying a glowstone. Their footsteps were soft and slow and uneven.

I rolled over and looked, found my bearings slowly in the dim green wash of the stone, and noticed immediately that the chamber hole was unblocked.

"Awake?" PaTri said. He limped toward me and thrust the glowstone into my face. "I'm told that you're afraid of the dark. Is that right?"

I glared at him.

"Poor thing," he gloated. "Can't see in the dark. But where you're going it is always dark!"

I gave him a suggestion so rude it would have made some of the kingsguard blush, using words that would not have made Father proud.

PaTri laughed cruelly, and then reached out with one finger and flicked the head of the thorn.

I screamed for a long moment before gritting my teeth.

"Such manners," he said. "And to think I was going to do you a favor. If you had only kept your mouth shut and gone quietly to Cadrid, you might have met your mother there."

I must have gawked, because he smiled again, wider this time. "Though of course she may not have survived her journey. The taskmasters were not so careful with their cargo back then. I remember her well. A thin, frail thing."

"You lie," I spat.

"Do I?" He shrugged. "What does it matter? Things have changed now. I have new plans for you. Queen IsaBel has authorized a special sacrifice for the Spring Festival. Guess who's invited?"

A special sacrifice meant blood. Mouse blood shed in an offering to Kalla, chief of the Cadridian gods.

My blood.

"Don't you feel honored?" He stood and limped back toward the chamber hole. At the entry he turned and said, "Soon, you will be Kalla's."

◆ ◆ ◆

Darkness returned immediately, though now it seemed even worse, for PaTri's glowstone had shrunk my pupils.

At least now I could locate the wall, and I scooted toward it as quickly as I could. Halfway there I brushed against one of the stacks of dried herbs, and all at once I knew where I was.

The knowledge inspired a bitter laugh. I should have realized sooner. I had been here before. PaTri had moved me to his own storage room in the temple of Kalla. I sniffed at the closest stack, recognizing the smell. The place was packed with maywort.

I thought, If I am going to die for something, I may as well do the deed. And though I won't recount the details, I did at last befoul a stack of maywort in the temple of Kalla. Probably more than a month's supply.

But I felt no satisfaction. I didn't have time. The shadows returned, from where I do not know. The shapes, the faces, the beings that Father sometimes referred to as lost souls.

PaTri thought I feared darkness for its own sake, because of what the darkness might hide. But that wasn't my problem at all. It was what the darkness *revealed* that terrified me.

It's not that I can't see in the dark. It's that I can.

Chapter Seven

Burnt Offering

"You mean you left it in, PaTri?" a voice I didn't recognize said. "That's barbaric! And, it's festering."

"How can you tell?" PaTri asked. His voice came from a distance.

"Does Kalla take your nose as well as your soul when you make your vows? It reeks."

"What does it matter? He's going to die anyway."

"Yes, and sooner than you think. That paw is infected."

Nausea rolled my stomach over.

I opened my eyes slowly, aware of the presence of a glowstone by the green edge of the darkness. Sweat matted my fur, ran in streams down my face.

An older mouse frowned down at me. "He's feverish. He won't last until the Spring Festival like this. Don't you know anything?"

"He deserves a little pain," PaTri said.

"Have you given him food? Water? Loosened his bonds every day?"

"Oh, he's watered. My own little flower sprouting here among the maywort. No food, of course, because I don't want him contaminating any more of the herbs."

"No, and I wager you haven't loosened those bonds even once. How did you expect him to last until the festival?"

"It's only another week."

"Only?" A cold paw pressed to my forehead, and I gasped. "Well. You may untie his paws. In his condition he won't be walking anywhere soon. I imagine you'll have to carry him to the river when the time comes. Hold this."

The older mouse passed his glowstone to PaTri and then stooped over my paws. "Ugh! Look at this, PaTri."

PaTri leaned over me and looked, his face expressionless.

"It's a wonder he's still alive." With one quick motion the old mouse ripped out the thorn, sending pain in red-hot waves through my paw, ankle, and thigh.

I screamed, but he wasn't done yet. He dumped cold water into the wound, then padded it with a clump of moss. Colors flashed before my wide-open eyes.

"Well, you've certainly killed him," the old mouse said. "Your little moment of revenge is going to cost you the Spring Festival. You'd better give him more water."

"He won't last another week?" PaTri sounded worried.

"Perhaps. But the odds are against him." The light of the glowstone faded as they moved to the door, and their voices grew faint. "It's obvious he doesn't want to live any more."

◆ ◆ ◆

When I awoke again I could move my paws freely. My left paw still felt as though it were punctured by the thorn. It burned with a ferocious pain.

I tried to stand, but never even made it to my knees. I had no strength. The old mouse was right; they needed no bonds to restrain me.

I had lost all track of time. It seemed to me that I had lain in the storage room for years. In reality, with the Spring Festival only a few days away, it must have been more like three weeks.

Mitts brought water in a curled leaf and left it by my head each morning. I kept my eyes closed and pretended to sleep when I heard him approach. He would set the water down and say, "Here you go, little slug," and then stomp out.

When he was gone, I would whisper, "Thanks, you giant cloud of gas fresh from a pig's backside." And one day Father's face appeared in my mind. In the darkness

I had grown used to all kinds of faces appearing. Not just lost souls, but those of memory and imagination as well.

"Was that appropriate?" Father asked.

"For him, no," I answered. "But all the appropriate descriptions involve words you never wanted me to use."

Several days after the thorn was removed, PaTri himself came into the chamber and glared at me. "Still alive, I see." He pinched the skin of my neck and felt for my pulse. "You know, you really are lucky. I can think of a hundred more painful ways to die than on the altar of sacrifice, any of which would suit me."

"I saw Kalla," I told him.

He stared at me coldly for a moment. "What are you babbling about?"

"Kalla. Your god. I see her sometimes in the darkness."

"You see him?" His expression blended curiosity and disbelief.

"Her. And the other lost souls. Some of them, anyway."

"You lie."

"What does it matter? Tomorrow I'll be dead."

He glanced at the open chamber hole, then stared back into my face. "What does he look like?" More than just curiosity now. Fascination. Fear. Eagerness.

I almost couldn't believe what I saw in his eyes. For all his training—his vows and sacrifices and years of service in the Temple of Kalla—he didn't really believe.

"She looks like a lizard," I said. "A cold, selfish lizard with dead eyes and the mouth of a fish."

Disbelief crossed his face. "Stupid boy."

"You asked," I said. "Someday you'll see her for yourself."

Fear crossed his face and he turned and stomped out of the chamber, leaving me again in darkness.

"I hope that day comes soon," I added.

But the next day was my day. The Spring Festival had arrived.

◆ ◆ ◆

They trussed me up again in the morning and ran a stick under the cords. Mitts grabbed one end of the stick and Spew the other.

"He looks smaller," Spew said.

They lifted the stick, with me tied to it, off the ground. I didn't have the strength to raise my head. It hung down, bobbing with each of their plodding steps.

"Light," Mitts said. "I expected him to be heavy."

"PaTri didn't want to waste food on him."

They carried me out of the temple area and into a dark corridor. Hanging from the stick, I saw the world upside down. The floor swayed above me. The dark curved walls of the Great Hall fell into darkness beneath.

They trudged up the ramp of the Common Gate, Spew complaining that he now carried the heavy end, and we emerged into sunlight. I shut my eyes against the force of it, let the sun burn for a moment through my eyelids.

The guards at the gate sang as I passed them, something I recognized. They always cheered the sacrifice on its way to the Rock. Their words followed us:

Here's to Kalla, quick and strong,
Who lends us speed to flee.

Life is short, and death is long.
Better him than me!

Mitts and Spew set me down outside the Common Gate and stood blinking in the bright light of the afternoon. The field above Tira-Nor lay bent under the heat of the day, the prairie grass brown and brittle.

The unseasonable heat awakened my fever. Sweat poured into my eyes as Mitts and Spew angled south and west, toward the saddle between Round Top and the claw's end of the Dark Forest. They stopped periodically to rest and dropped me twice climbing down into Dry Gully. My back hit a stone and I cried out, which drew a sneer from Mitts.

"Quit griping. We're doing all the work."

"Trade you," I tried to say. But the words fell weak from my lips, and he didn't hear me.

I closed my eyes and told myself that PaTri was right. I could imagine worse things than dying on the Rock.

Living. That would be worse.

Father's face appeared in my mind. Sadness hung on him like a weight, as it had the day Mother disappeared. His voice sounded like the wind in the summer grass. *"Run."*

Crowds of mice lined the north bank of the White River. They cheered as we passed down the long trail through Dry Gully and onto the stony clutter of the river floor. Thick, murky pools stood along the riverbed between bleached stones. At the south bank a narrow trickle of oily water gurgled its way west.

On the north bank, where the river's edge rose up into a high wall over the gully, stood King Ahaz and

Queen IsaBel. Around them, the royal courtiers chatted and nibbled on bits of food carried by slaves from the palace hall.

PaTri, too, stood on the north bank, but below the royal train. He had smeared his fur with mud from the river, which gave him a dark, unnatural look. Around him, almost two dozen Cadridian priests gathered in the shadow of a root that jutted from the bank.

Mitts and Spew slowed their pace. They measured their steps and jumped in unison when going from stone to stone. Perhaps they wanted to look dignified. More likely they feared slipping into the pools.

Our destination lay in the middle of the riverbed, a large rock shaped like a snout angling upward from the earth. Father told me once that TyMin had dubbed the rock "Whiskers," and had even drawn black lines across its surface the day he led the Ancients out of their slavery and into the Known Lands.

Mitts and Spew carried me around to the far side, out of sight of the north bank, and set me down to catch their breath.

"Don't suppose you could crawl up?" Mitts said, huffing.

"Sure," I managed. "You can just leave me here."

Spew gave me a halfhearted kick and looked at Mitts. He jerked his head to the top of the rock. "Half my feast ration if you take the down side."

Mitts considered the offer for a moment. "Done."

The pitch on this side of the Rock made the climb possible, but not easy. I hung swaying from the stick under searing heat as the sun marched higher.

Spew crested the rock first, then turned and grabbed me under the armpits and pulled. Mitts came panting over the edge and collapsed near me.

I lay next to a bundle of sticks arranged in a cone above a loose bird's nest of dried grass. Across the river, someone pointed toward us, and mice began to stream to the riverbank to watch.

Spew took a deep breath and said, "Let's get on with it." He produced a length of cord from behind a pile of wood. They tilted me upright against the cone and tied the stick at top and bottom.

In the distance, above the high bank, something glinted like a thousand suns, sharp as a knife in my eyes.

Mitts saw my look and grinned. "That'd be the glass."

Spew crumpled a handful of dried maywort over my head. "I hope you like heat."

They turned and disappeared over the lip of the rock.

The Cadridians began to chant, a long, low sound, wordless and indistinguishable. Working together, they raised the fire-glass on its shaft. PaTri adjusted the angle as the sound of their chanting filled the riverbed.

Faces stared out at me from the riverbank, and as I closed my eyes against them, they were replaced by more faces—from the oily black of the water, from the dark shapes of trees at the horizon, from the darker shadows of my memory.

"Son," Father said. *"What are you doing here?"*

"Dying."

"Why?"

"Because I am not Glyn the Strong," I said. "I haven't the strength to resist them."

"You don't need strength," Father said. *"Just desire. Do you want to live?"*

"No."

"Do you want to resist them?"

"I don't know."

"Then look, Son. Look!"

I opened my eyes, saw a long line of slaves snaking down Dry Gully from the field above Tira-Nor, their backs mounded with stores of food they would not be allowed to eat. Compassion rose in my heart, side-by-side with spite. I felt as though I were split in two. One Eli thought, *No one deserves a life of slavery*. The other Eli thought, *What a stupid thing to think. At least they're alive! None of them is about to be burned to death.*

"You can save them," Father whispered in my ear. *"You only have to want to."*

I tugged weakly at the cords that bound my wrists to the stick. "*Want to* is all I have."

I turned my head, took a deep breath, and inhaled a lungful of black fear that curled from the dried grass and bracken all around me. Smoke rose from the Rock in a long finger pointing at heaven.

Chapter Eight

Glyn the Strong

When Glyn reached the age of enlistment, his father took him to RuHoff's cave. Sir Lyn carried two raisins wrapped in a willow leaf. He told Glyn to stand in a shaft of light and count dust motes. Then Lyn lay on his back in the center of the cavern and stared at the figures etched into the ceiling.

After a little while, Glyn's voice rang out in the dim light. "Finished!"

His father rose to one elbow. "What do you mean, finished?"

"Counting," Glyn said. "You told me to count the dust motes. There are six thousand one hundred twenty-two."

His father lay back down. "You can't have counted them already," he said. "There are too many."

"How do you know? Did you count them?"

"Start over."

"But this is boring!"

"True," said Sir Lyn. "But I thought you wanted to be strong."

"I am strong."

"Strong enough to count dust motes?"

Glyn cocked his head to one side. "Counting doesn't take strength."

"Oh? And what does it take?"

Glyn tapped one finger against his lips. He knew his father never asked meaningless questions. After a moment, he said, "Time."

"Exactly," Lyn said. "Which is why I told you to count dust motes. You may be strong. You may be brilliant. You may be rich, wise, powerful, quick, or even fearless. ElShua's gifts come in many sizes and flavors, but time is the same for every mouse. It is a gift no one ever receives in abundance. True strength will come when you understand how short life is. Come lie here beside me for a moment."

Glyn ambled over to his father and plopped down. "What are we doing here?"

"We are growing. You, by counting dust motes; I, by trying to make sense of these pictures."

"Why?"

"Because we are noblemice, and it is the duty and privilege of nobles to unravel puzzles. Just as it is our duty to right wrongs and defend the weak."

"Must we always unravel them?" Glyn asked. "What if I sometimes feel like *raveling* a puzzle? What if I want to make, not just unmake?"

Sir Lyn laughed. "RuHoff the Wise was a raveler. You could do worse than emulating him."

Glyn looked up at the ceiling. "Why was he called RuHoff the Wise? Surely there were other wise mice in Tira-Nor when he lived. Did anyone ever call him just RuHoff?"

"His wisdom was like a great deed. Something so extraordinary that it defined him. I suppose one could not think of the name RuHoff without also thinking of the word *wise*. Though I have often heard that his contemporaries grew so tired of hearing him called wise that they expelled him from the city. That's when he came to live here."

"And when he wrote his riddles?"

"I suppose."

Glyn said, "I would not like to always be called wise."

"No?"

"I would like to be called strong. Glyn the Strong."

Lyn eyed the boy's muscular frame. "How strong must you be for that to happen? How strong is strong enough?"

Glyn smiled slowly and rose. "Be right back," he said. He darted out of the cave and returned a few minutes later carrying a rock twice the size of his head. He held it out in one paw as though it were a mulberry. "I am the only mouse in Tira-Nor who can do this," he said. He turned the rock over so that it hung suspended under the grip of his fingers. "And I'm not even trying." He let go.

Sir Lyn felt the heavy thud of earth against his back as dust swirled. He whistled. "Yes, son, you are very strong. Tell me something. Are you hungry?"

"Ravenous."

He stood and unwrapped the parcel he had been using for a pillow. "Raisin?" he asked, holding it out in one paw.

Glyn stared at him, his eyes wide. "But, Father! You know I mustn't eat raisins."

"Indeed I do, Son." He wrapped the raisin back in the leaf. "I just wondered if you did."

Glyn blinked. His gaze wandered to the bulging willow leaf. "Are they tasty?"

"They are," Sir Lyn said. "But not as tasty as strength."

Glyn turned and faced the cave entrance. After a long time, he said, "You were wrong about the dust motes."

"What's that?"

"I did count them when you told me to. There really were six thousand one hundred twenty-two." He pointed at the rock. "But there are more now."

Chapter Nine

One Friend Richer

Heat collected on my palms, wrapping around my arms as the fire crackled behind me. I tugged against the stick, but it didn't budge.

Shouts erupted from the mice on the north bank. One of the Cadridians pointed to the plateau on the opposite slope of Dry Gully. A mouse stood there, his fur lit by the setting sun, his frame wiry as an old weed.

King Ahaz rose and thundered to the slope, one paw cupped above his eyes, his frown visible even from my position on the Rock. "Traitor!" he shouted.

"This is your fault! You made this drought! You killed the river and stopped up the clouds. And you have the audacity to show yourself now?" He kicked at the earth and sent a little tuft of dust rising into the air. "How dare you come here!"

The mice craned their necks to stare at the figures above them. None dared even a whisper.

"My fault?" AlBaer asked, his eyebrows raised.

"Don't try to deny it," Ahaz fumed. "It is your curse that haunts the Known Lands."

AlBaer spread out his paws to the mice below him as though waiting for the stragglers in the gully to collect themselves at the edges of the crowd. "Of course I will not deny it. But I am surprised at you, Majesty. Do you mean to tell us that you believe in ElShua, after all?"

Ahaz's jaw hung down. His face reddened.

Queen IsaBel appeared at the king's side. "You may keep your curses and your wit, Seer," she said. "ElShua has abandoned us. Why should we serve him?"

The warmth at my wrists grew as the fire in the bird's nest burst to life. A long line of heat rose along my back up to my neck.

AlBaer looked away from the king and queen, staring into the upturned faces of the slaves in the gully below. "You must serve someone. Kalla has brought you only blood and misery."

"Blood?" The queen's eyes flashed. She pointed across the river to me. "Blood will bring us water."

"Majesties." AlBaer took a deep breath. He looked into my eyes for the first time, and I saw that he wasn't smiling now. "I know you speak from ignorance of both ElShua and Kalla. But I have come to remedy that. I am here to make you a wager."

King Ahaz scowled. "What sort of wager?"

"A duel to the death. ElShua versus Kalla. With Tira-Nor as the spoils of combat. Whoever wins will be Lord of the Known Lands."

"*I* am Lord of the Known Lands," Ahaz said.

"Yet you cannot make it rain." AlBaer looked up into the cloudless sky.

The king's face reddened still more deeply and he seemed to struggle for something to say.

Queen IsaBel glided forward to the edge of Dry Gully. "You dare to mock the king?"

AlBaer ignored her. "My Lord," he said, staring directly at Ahaz, "every mortal mouse has his limits. I am here only to demonstrate what you have never known." He raised one bony finger in the air, then slowly lowered it until it pointed directly at the Cadridians standing in the shadow of the root. "What they have never known."

A brief feeling of strength surged through my spine as fear gripped me. I kept my tail as far from the heat as I could, but soon my back would catch and then nothing could save me. Odd. A moment ago I thought I wanted to die. Now . . .

PaTri apparently could not see the reaction of the king and queen, who stood directly above him. He stepped forward out of shadow and craned his neck. "My Lord?" he called.

AlBaer did not wait for the king to speak. His challenge sounded like a snarl. "You have brought fire to the innocent, PaTri. This is a sure sign that Kalla is near. You have brought blood but not water."

I pulled against the stick, straining to put distance between my back and the fearsome heat of the fire. The frame of the cone shuddered and creaked, but did not move.

Glyn would have heaved the whole wood stack into the river. But not me.

PaTri said, "Kalla will come."

AlBaer's eyes narrowed. "King Ahaz, I said I would make you a wager. And I shall. I will sacrifice twenty-three mice by the teeth of ElShua this day. And I will do so before PaTri and his brethren sacrifice even one."

On the riverbank a Cadridian priest raised his fist to AlBaer. "What do you mean? There are twenty-three of us. Do you make threats?"

"Threats?" AlBaer said. "No. I won't raise a finger against you. I won't need to. ElShua will deal with you, and then you will have to deal with Kalla. I have no doubt who will get the smaller bite of that crumb."

Ahaz looked across the river at me as the light from the fire grew. A look of puzzlement crossed his face. "What are the stakes?"

"When ElShua answers, you must give the boy to me." Again his gaze shot across the river to where I stood straining against my bonds.

Ahaz smiled. "And if he doesn't answer, will you leave the Known Lands forever?"

AlBaer drew himself up and stretched out both front paws toward the river. "There is no chance of that."

Something exploded behind me. Light and heat flashed around my head, searing my neck, shoving me forward and down. Twigs and blackened chunks of wood gouged the sky in streaks, trailing smoke. Cinders shot through the air like stars, orange against the dark clouds billowing outward.

The explosion severed the bonds at my wrists and shattered the stick to which I had been tied. A short stump of wood lay across my lower back, and I fell to all fours, staring down as a sensation of delicious coolness moved down my shoulders and onto my back.

The mice in Dry Gully stood stiffly, as though incapable of movement. No one panicked. No one ran. No one even looked away. They stared transfixed, every eye looking up at the Rock, at me.

My legs trembled, though I felt no pain. *This is what it's like to die,* I thought. *To pass into the spirit realm. AlBaer's lost his wager.*

The noise of the explosion died away as pieces of charred wood fell to earth in a wide circle around me.

I stared, amazed. Everywhere the wood hit remnant puddles of water, steam plumed upward in a white arc, followed by shafts of fire. Dozens of tiny volcanoes spouted from the murky, black pools, from the slick surfaces of rock, from the trickle of the river itself. The columns of fire bent sideways and began to pour themselves into lines. They forked like lightning and joined themselves into veins that danced and crackled north toward the bank of the river.

We all watched. The king and queen. AlBaer. The mice of the Commons. The slaves still loitering stoop-shouldered under their loads of food. The Cadridians, whose mouths opened stupidly.

The lines of fire merged into a semicircle around PaTri and his priests, then rose in a sheet and surged slowly toward the center, like the pincers of a giant insect.

That's not natural, I thought, too stunned to think anything but obvious thoughts. *That's not what fire does.*

All at once the priests sprang into action. Behind the flames they clawed frantically at the cliff wall. One of them screamed, and I looked away toward Dry Gully.

The mice of the city had found their senses. They streamed away in a long line, the slaves throwing off their burdens, the mice of the Commons shoving and kicking at each other in desperation.

Above Dry Gully, AlBaer turned in a tight circle, knees pumping, shoulders wagging, his face split by a grin. "Come again later!" he shouted. "Come again later! Ha ha!"

The cool feeling along my back only increased, and for a moment I glanced upward, because I felt as though I were standing under a waterfall, and I thought that certainly rain had come at last. But there were no clouds, and the sun still stood on the horizon.

I turned and stumbled around the edge of the black circle where the fire had been, my legs wobbly, wondering where I would find the strength to get down off the Rock. The nerves in my thorn-punctured paw stabbed fire into my leg.

I collapsed onto my back, gasping.

◆ ◆ ◆

A few moments later AlBaer stood on the Rock with me, smiling down gently, his eyes watery. He touched my wounded paw with one finger. A tingling sensation flowed into my paw, delicious as sugar dissolving on the tongue. The pain vanished. "Better?"

I nodded.

"You'll find you have more strength now too." He pulled me upright with one scrawny arm, and I wondered why I had ever thought him weak. I rose feeling strangely well.

"Yes?" he asked.

Again I nodded. I think I pulled away from him, for his smile faded for a moment, as though he were hurt.

I couldn't help myself. He terrified me.

He touched my shoulder with one paw, as if to steady me. "Cheer up, young Eli. This morning you were entirely friendless and condemned to death by fire. Now you are one friend richer." He smiled. "And I am condemning you to life."

Chapter Ten

Apprentice

Anger boiled in my veins. "Life? Life?!"

His smile disintegrated slowly. His eyes moved like fingers working a puzzle. "You are . . . angry?"

I backed away from him. He had healed my paw. He had rescued me from being burned alive. He had purchased my freedom and spoken kindly to me. And yet—

"Say thank you," Father whispered in my head.

"No!"

AlBaer's head tilted to one side. "No?"

"No, I won't say thank you."

He shrugged and waved one paw in the direction of the field. "No matter. Why should you be any different from the rest of them?"

"Different?" Guilt and rage fought for control of my mouth. Guilt lost, suddenly and irrevocably. Perhaps it surrendered. Rage settled on my shoulders like an old blanket. "I am different! I was the one they tried to kill, not you. I was the one tied up in PaTri's storage chamber. I was the one with a thorn in my paw! What did you do?"

"Excuse me," AlBaer said, his back very straight. "Perhaps your brain cooked in the fire and you don't remember. I stopped them."

"Don't . . ." Father said.

I clenched my fists. "You stopped them? You *stopped them*! You mean you could have stopped them but *didn't*! You were too busy. Come again later, you said. He isn't a seer, you said. And then, best of all, the king is a twit. Tell him that for me. That was brilliant! Do you know what they did to him?"

"Him?" AlBaer's voice fell into the air like a dandelion seed. "Your father?"

"Eli," Father whispered. *"Please don't. It's not his fault."*

I ignored him. What did Father know anyway? He was just a voice in my head. Every time I listened to his voice I saw his silhouette—an outline and nothing more. A shape that grew darker and emptier as details fell from it like clumps of fur. I couldn't stand the thought of Father's forgiveness extending even to this crazy old mouse. I didn't want Father to forgive him.

"Do you know?" I screamed at AlBaer as a dark shadow swept over us. "Do you? Because I thought you were supposed to be a seer. And you said ElShua was going to promote him. But that didn't happen, did it? *Did it*?!"

AlBaer's shoulders drooped.

For some reason this made me even angrier. "No," I said, chest heaving. "It didn't happen. They just killed him. While all the others—" My voice caught in my throat. "While they—" I couldn't get the words out. My anger died away to a sudden, sick feeling of loneliness. All at once I couldn't think about AlBaer any more, even though he stood there in front of me like a wire statue.

He let out a long sigh, his eyes glistening, and nodded as though he understood.

Something big and wet like a bird dropping spattered the rock behind me. "They laughed about it," I said. "When they killed him. They laughed."

He kept nodding, even though he no longer looked at me. He stood there gazing down into the charred remains of the fire, as though searching for something very small, something that was perhaps not even there. "They would do something like that. How horrible it must be to live in their skin."

This statement hit me in the gut like a fist.

"Poor blind fools," he said. "You are going to have to help them."

"Me?" I protested. "I'm not going to help them."

"Not today, no. Today is a day for running. And, I think, a day for getting wet." He looked up into the sky and held out one paw, palm up, as heavy raindrops fell *plap-plap-plap* all around us. "We will have to hurry or be swept away by the current. Are you coming?"

◆ ◆ ◆

I hadn't noticed the storm clouds rolling in. Before we had made it down the slope of the Rock, they covered the sky, boiling black and heavy with magic. I felt this before I understood it. The fur on the back of my neck bristled.

How did the storm hurl itself across the sky with no wind at all behind it? What kind of power did AlBaer possess?

The skies opened before we finished climbing the north bank of the river. Huge drops spattered my face and struck the ground like ripe berries. Static wove itself through the air, though for the moment I felt no fear. It was difficult to be afraid of anything while standing next to AlBaer.

I crested the plateau and inhaled the clean-air smell of rain in great heaves. The stench of herbs and blood and madness from PaTri's storage chamber still coated my nostrils, fine as a layer of dust, but it was washing away. My paws tingled with newfound strength.

The thought of PaTri's chamber prompted me to turn and look down into the riverbed, where the trickle of water had already risen to tumble over the smaller rocks and pools.

PaTri.

On the north bank, just visible from where we stood, was the spot where the Cadridians had died. Nothing remained but a dark smear against the river wall, a shadow with indistinct, grasping claws. As I watched, rainwater spilling down the steep bank drew the slag-shape down, toward the river, in long black streaks.

Standing behind me, AlBaer patted my shoulder as I tried to catch my breath.

I pointed. "How did you do that?" I asked.

"Do what?" He stepped forward and peered down into the river.

I wagged my finger at the blackened root for emphasis. "That. The fire. The priests. PaTri! That was *amazing*!"

AlBaer's smile faded. He stared at me as though he hadn't understood the question, then slowly shook his head. "And you called me crazy." He turned and headed through the grass.

"Wait a minute." I started after him, but he was already way ahead of me. I felt like a kit again. I had to jog to match his quiet, long-legged stride. For a crazy old strip of leather as thin as a pine needle, AlBaer could really move.

"Why should I wait?" he called back, "when it is raining like this, and I know a dry place where I can sleep safely with no one asking me silly questions?"

"What's going on?" I said this to his rear end, which was all I could see of him, not counting the strip of wire he called a tail.

"Come again later."

"Quit saying that!" I shouted. He must have heard me, but he kept going, even though I had stopped. He was climbing the gently sloping field west of Dry Gully, and it didn't take long for him to disappear behind a curtain of rain and brown-bladed grass.

Whatever anger I felt about the phrase "come again later" apparently couldn't survive the rain. I stood dripping with cold water as the clouds rumbled overhead and the river began to surge behind me. It would be dark soon.

I looked in the direction of Tira-Nor, but the gate holes weren't visible from this distance. I doubted the sentries would be out anyway. Even Grayfeather, the crippled hawk who usually perched on the lone oak above Round Top, seemed to have retreated to whatever shelter he called home.

"Father?" I said aloud. "Are you here?"

No answer. That figured.

I sat down into the squishing soil, feeling more lonely than I had even in PaTri's chamber. I looked up into clouds the color of the moss that grows in the heart of the Dark Forest and let water pelt my face. Some of it touched my lips, awakening my thirst. I tilted my head back and let the rain spatter into my open mouth.

Mitts hadn't brought me a water ration this morning, probably deeming it unnecessary given the circumstances. I wondered if he had survived AlBaer's burst of fire magic, and at last decided he must have, because I couldn't recall seeing him among the Cadridians gathered around PaTri. Neither Mitts nor Spew were full priests yet. Since they hadn't formally said their vows, they wouldn't have been standing in the inner circle.

Too bad, I thought, and then felt a twinge of conscience.

The water was heavenly. It fell slowly but steadily, washing the grime from my throat and seeping into the emptiness of my body. How could I have been so thirsty and not have realized it?

"Feeling better?"

I opened my eyes. AlBaer sat next to me, his mouth open to the sky, but his eyes very much fixed on me. I hadn't heard him approach, and his arrival—though oddly not surprising—was eerie nonetheless. I looked away, back toward the moss roiling overhead.

"You left." I shot him an accusing look.

"You shtocked," he said, his mouth still open. "And I cang dack."

I couldn't argue with that. Besides, looking at him with his mouth open, I didn't really want to.

"So what now?" I asked. "What am I supposed to do?"

A look of surprise flitted across his face. He closed his mouth and shook his head, sending water out in a flat spray. "That is an excellent question, Eli. One that—" He grinned and poked me in the shoulder with one crooked finger, emphasizing each word: "—too—few—mice—ever—ask."

"Ow."

"It is customary in such arrangements for an apprentice to do what he is told."

"Apprentice?" I asked, rubbing my shoulder.

"I won you fair and square. You belong to me. You will serve as my apprentice until it is time for me to move on. Then you shall take my place."

"I thought you didn't need an apprentice."

"And I thought you'd rather be sold to the Cadridians." He stared at me with inscrutable eyes, whiskers twitching. "An arrangement that could still be managed if necessary." His smile flickered.

By the throne, he's serious. I thought. He would do it. He would sell me back into slavery! But if he had wanted to do that, he wouldn't have offered to make me an apprentice.

Did I want the job? That was the question. Apprentice was probably no better than slave, when it came down to it. Both amounted to doing someone else's heavy lifting, and taking orders without raising too much fuss. What did it matter what it was called if it meant the same thing?

But they didn't mean the same thing, and I knew it. Father would not have asked AlBaer to make me his slave.

I had the strange feeling that AlBaer could see the thoughts running circles in my head like ants, and was waiting for one of them to win. I ought to have accepted his offer graciously, but I didn't, though I had no alternative. Where could I have gone? How would I have lived? And what did it mean that I could see things—creatures and shapes and events—that others couldn't see? Was this what it meant to be a seer? Or was being a seer something one could be taught, like how to hide or fight?

I didn't answer his question; neither did I ask a sensible question. Something stood in the way, like a tree I couldn't see around.

"I asked first," I said stubbornly. "You said you didn't need an apprentice. You said I'd only slow you down."

"True," he admitted. "But things change. Your father stood up to them. And it seems I have even less time than I had thought. Which means someone must take my place. Someone must demonstrate the power of mercy. Someone must free the mice of Tira-Nor and end this ridiculous slave trade with Cadrid." He stared at me thoughtfully. "That is, if I can find anyone up to the job."

"What do you mean, free the mice of Tira-Nor? Are you talking about the ones in Cadrid?"

"Slavery isn't only doing someone else's bidding.

It is an attitude. The mice of Tira-Nor are enslaved and they don't even know it."

"Why can't you free them?"

"I told you, I won't be here when the time comes."

"Where are you going?"

"Away."

"Apparently, you don't have to tell me."

"Correct!" AlBaer smiled. "But that doesn't mean I won't. When the time is right." He looked up into the sky. "Not that I mind the rain, but shall we go somewhere a skosh more dry? It's a long walk."

We stood. My legs were coated in mud, though AlBaer's were surprisingly clean. How had he managed that?

"You never told me how you did that thing at the river. You know, with the fire?"

His expression soured instantly. "That's the second time you've brought that up. Why would you ask such a question?"

"Why?" I stared at him as though he'd grown an extra tail. "Why wouldn't I? If I'm to be your apprentice—if I'm to take your place—don't I need to know what you know? What if I have to blast the Cadridians one day and you aren't around?"

He drew a deep breath and grumbled a few words I couldn't understand. After a pause he said, "Your paw is healed. Your strength and freedom are returned to you. But all you can think about is how to kill and destroy."

Now I knew he was crazy. "What good is power you never use? Someone taught you, right? You can't just make up miracles out of your mind."

He shook his head, muttering, "Out of your mind."

"What?" I asked.

"The miracle isn't what I did. It's that you missed it, even though it centered on you."

"I didn't miss it," I protested. "I saw the whole thing."

"You? Saw?" He let out a long sigh, as though coming to a decision. "I'm going to leave you now. I will not sell you to the Cadridians, because that would be a very wicked thing to do. Nor will I force you to be my apprentice. I am freeing you from any unlikely feeling of debt or gratitude you may have toward me for saving your life. Consider us even. The world—" he spread his paws expansively, "—is your raisin. Go where you wish, though I suggest you avoid Queen IsaBel, and therefore Tira-Nor. You might find a future in the Houses of Men. You might scrabble out a decent life in the Dark Forest. The choice is yours. Good luck." He started to walk off, then turned and added, "I am sorry about your father. He was a rare mouse. Good in the midst of evil. You might learn something from him if you try."

He turned again and stalked away.

I waited just long enough to feel how completely alone I was, except for Grayfeather, who had resumed his perch atop the hill.

Then I followed AlBaer north.

Chapter Eleven

Oracles

I woke to a steady drizzle. Morning light, filtered by storm clouds, muddled up from the opening of RuHoff's cave. I stared at the sloped ceiling and blinked awake to the rhythm of rain pelting the turf outside.

I didn't recognize the symbols at first. Dark shapes zigzagged across the rough ceiling, groups of paw prints that were divided into smaller patterns. Each print stood separated from the others by a narrow space of blank rock so that the ceiling almost looked like a cluster of painted islands.

I thought I could see a difference in the way some of the islands were etched, which only made sense. RuHoff was not the only mouse to stamp ideas into the rock. Glyn the Strong had left behind some of his more powerful riddles to tease future generations. It was said that only one mouse in ten thousand could decode the secret pictures.

"Nonsense," Father whispered.

I agreed. If only one in ten thousand learned to read the pictures it was because the others didn't care what the pictures meant.

AlBaer lay curled into a skinny ball of fur in the far corner. His snore came high-pitched from his snout, almost a giggle against the steady sound of rain.

I reached up with one paw but couldn't touch the ceiling. I padded over to where AlBaer lay and let out a long sigh just above his head. The snoring stopped.

When he didn't move for a long time, I hunkered down closer and sighed again. Still nothing. He almost looked dead. Come to think of it, he had told me he was leaving soon. But he'd been snoring just a few moments ago. Surely the old nut wouldn't die like that.

Would he?

I reached out with one finger and poked him in the shoulder.

One eye opened halfway in an unspoken accusation. "What?"

"Are you awake?"

Still he didn't move. The eyelid snapped shut like a door slamming. "No."

"But I want to ask you something."

"Later."

"Please?"

"Later!"

I sighed and looked out through the low entrance. I wasn't going anywhere until the rain let up anyway. "I guess it can wait."

I poked around for a while, trying not to make too much noise, and eventually found a narrow ledge deep in the heart of the cave. Just beneath it a crack opened. Dim light spilled from the crack, revealing a low crawl space between two sheets of rock that stretched for several body lengths. I stared into it, wondering if it could be Glyn's "hall of revelation." I had always pictured the tunnel bigger. How could a great muscular warrior fit into such a low space? It looked almost large enough for me to wiggle through, but I wasn't Glyn the Strong, and I wouldn't have crawled into it for anything.

I retreated to my straw pallet and lay back to stare at the etchings. Father had always loved RuHoff best, but he often humored me with stories about Glyn. He had taught me as many of Glyn's riddles as he knew, but there were hundreds more I'd never heard.

Most of the markings weren't Glyn's, and so didn't interest me. RuHoff may have been wise, but I didn't need wisdom. I needed power. Besides, I had never paid all that much attention to the sayings of RuHoff. I doubted I could decipher any of his words.

The old and the young have this in common:
neither has long to live.

I sat up straight. Where had that come from? Some distant memory perhaps, or a story told in the Great

Hall by one of the Tellers? It surely wasn't one of Glyn's sayings. It had no character to it, no wit. It sounded like RuHoff.

Another tumbled into my mind, unbidden.

Pride is the exclusive privilege of the ignorant.

And then another.

Even the traitor serves his country.
He gives the thief a measure of dignity.

I stared up at the ceiling. Pride? Ignorance? Dignity? Those had to be oracles of RuHoff the Wise. Father had always liked the stories of RuHoff. I had pretended not to find them dull. But why was I remembering them now? Was it because I was here? Did the cave have some mystical effect on those who entered it? Or was it just a trick of my mind?

I glanced over at AlBaer and watched as his back rose and fell. He was snoring again—happily, it seemed to me.

Perhaps the oracles had something to do with him. Maybe the old coot was starting to rub off on me. Or was I just going weasel-crazy, like him?

Difficult? No. It is not difficult to get
what you want from ElShua.
You only have to change what you want.

That almost sounded like AlBaer.

I leaned back and concentrated on an individual

island of paw prints, the smallest island visible, two lonely lines that curved around a thin crack in the ceiling. The first mark—six lines shooting out from an empty space at the center—might have been sunbeams, but without a sun. Were they RuHoff's way of drawing light? Air? Wind? They looked like whiskers more than anything else, but whiskers with no face.

A thought struck me, intense in its clarity. Why must whiskers have a face? If you mean to draw whiskers, you draw whiskers.

I cycled through the etchings, some of which repeated themselves, then noticed that those on the bottom line faced the opposite direction of those on top. Did it matter what direction they faced? Were the etchings meant to be understood by all, or were they a kind of code designed to be understood only by a few—by the initiated?

That didn't fit what I knew about RuHoff. In the stories Father told, RuHoff always harped on about truth. Why take the time to record your almighty wisdom if you don't want people to understand it? Why disguise a message intended for everyone?

The answer hit me. And just like that the words etched in the ceiling took shape in my mind. I do not say that I figured it out. I didn't. In truth, I stumbled on the solution. The plain meaning of the etching stood before me naked as a newborn kit. RuHoff hadn't disguised anything. He had made it plain.

"I see it!" I shouted.

I see it! I see it! My voice came back, rolling off the rock walls like distant thunder and mixing with the rain.

AlBaer's snoring stopped. I felt his one open eye glare at me for silence.

How many times had I heard Father quote this same phrase? And here it was, written out in two short lines right over my head.

"What do you see?" AlBaer asked.

I shot him a triumphant smile and pointed. "I know what this means."

He squinted. "Are you sure? That one isn't Glyn's."

"No, it's RuHoff. Father used to quote it to me."

AlBaer rose, stretched, and sidled up next to me. "What do you think it says?"

Something about his expression drained away my confidence, which irritated me. "I don't just think I know what it says. I do know what it says."

"Really?"

"Yes."

"You're positive?"

"Yes."

"And how do you know something like that?"

I tried to explain what had happened as I lay there. I told him about the oracles I remembered, and about Father telling me stories of RuHoff the Wise, and how the thought of RuHoff writing in code had triggered something in my memory. I told him RuHoff hadn't written in code. He meant for his message to be read. Otherwise, why write anything at all?

AlBaer stared at me without comment.

That was unnerving. I wanted to tell AlBaer that I knew something else. I knew why he didn't have any friends. Instead, I finished with a shrug. "I can't explain it."

"On the contrary, you just did."

His eyes twinkled. Was he laughing at me? "But you haven't told me what you know. You've told me something more important. You've told me what you believe. So tell me, Eli. What do you believe it says?"

I looked at the tiny paw prints chasing each other in a circle overhead. "'Wroth sells disguises.'"

His gaze flicked to the ceiling. When he spoke, his voice came as a whisper. "Indeed he does. And mice buy them with their freedom. Which is why there must be seers."

Chapter Twelve

Quest

The rain ended like a pleasant dream. I couldn't tell exactly when it happened, but there was a moment, as I squatted in the mouth of the cave, when I knew the rain was past. The sun stabbed through the afternoon clouds and slashed the earth with long streaks. Green smells rose from the turf. The distant churning of the White River drifted up from the south, a heavier sound than the short-lived splash of rainwater funneling through Dry Gully.

I drew a deep breath and stared at my healed paw, tracing the long jagged scar left by PaTri's thorn, then looked up at the black and silver clouds.

AlBaer plopped down next to me. "You wanted to ask me a question?"

"Before I figured out the ceiling. Yes, I had a question. It doesn't make a lot of sense though."

"Here I am."

"PaTri said something when I was in the storage room. I didn't believe him, but now I can't stop thinking about it."

"What did he say?"

"That my mother was a slave in Cadrid. He said she might still be alive. But that's not really possible, right? Most slaves don't survive the trip, and the ones who do never live long."

AlBaer motioned with one paw as though shooing a fly. "Slavery in any form is evil. And yet, the Cadridians are not stupid. They spend a good deal on their slaves. It is the males who are sometimes worked to death, and then only as a punishment. Females are not sent to the docks."

Panic rose in my gut. A terrible feeling of having missed out on something important fought with my own incredulity. "Then it might be true? She might be alive?"

"It is possible, yes. But I do not say it is likely. It is also possible that PaTri was lying to you in order to toy with you. If he did send her to Cadrid, she may very well have passed on by now."

"But . . ." I couldn't think. "Where would I find her?"

"Find her?"

"How would I go about it? I've never been to Cadrid. Once I got there, where would I look? I have to do something."

"And what do you propose to do?"

"You said it was my job to end slavery. Why must I begin in Tira-Nor? Why not begin in Cadrid?"

"That may be more difficult than you imagine. If I know anything about the king of Cadrid—and I believe I do—he will make a show of force against Tira-Nor in a matter of weeks."

"Why?"

He pointed north. "Word will reach Cadrid that their emissaries are dead."

"Emissaries? You mean PaTri? The priests?"

AlBaer nodded. "They were guests of King Ahaz. According to Cadridian tradition, he should have protected them. Cadrid will want restitution."

I scratched my head. "What does that mean?"

"If I know Cadrid, it means more slaves. And if they cannot get that, they will want blood. Either way, I doubt they would treat you well."

"But I didn't do anything," I protested.

"You lived," he said simply, "when you were supposed to die."

"But you did that, not me."

Again he nodded. "True."

"How is that fair?"

AlBaer wetted one finger in his mouth and held it up in the air. "Fair?" He sniffed. "It isn't fair. Why would you ask such a foolish question? I smell dandelion."

He stepped into the sunlight, nose twitching, and I reluctantly followed.

By the time I caught up with him he was chewing thoughtfully on a yellow petal. "A little early," he said. "But not unsatisfying. Help yourself, Eli."

The smell of food awakened my stomach. How many days had it been since I had last eaten anything? I couldn't remember.

"Slow down," AlBaer said. "Your stomach will have shrunk."

Later, we lay on the open field under a swarm of gnats. "I have to find out what happened to her. Even if she is dead, I have to know."

AlBaer considered this. He lay on his chest, hands folded under his chin. "I agree."

"Really?"

"Better to know than always wonder. And if she is alive," he said, "she will be very glad to see you. A mother would be foolish that way."

The thought of seeing my mother again lit a warm, happy feeling in my chest, though I knew it was unlikely. Somehow the fact that AlBaer considered it possible made it feel more like an established fact.

"How long will it take for word to reach Cadrid?"

He snorted. "You can't outrun it, if that's what you're thinking. Bad news—"

"Why not?" I said, rising to my knees.

"Because you can't. As I was saying, bad news runs faster than any mouse."

"Not faster than Glyn the Strong. He once ran to Cadrid and back in half a day."

"That was different, Eli."

"Different how?"

He scowled. "He was Glyn the Strong, for one thing."

"You couldn't do it?"

"Me?" He looked surprised.

"AlBaer the Wise, the Merciful, Grand Seer of Tira-Nor, Maker of Miracles and Potentate Secundi Propositum. Could you do it if you wanted to?"

"I might be able to do such a thing." He stroked his chin. "But it would take more than wanting to. It would take a miracle. And I don't even want to."

"You don't have to want to. You just have to want me to."

He laughed suddenly. "Now I begin to see the makings of an apprentice. However, you are wrong. Any miracle I gave you would not last past the first whisper of doubt you heard between here and there. The miracle would have to come from you. Just like the wanting."

"Then tell me how to make a miracle!"

He sat silent for a long time. When he spoke, his voice had changed. It was low and level and somehow both old and young at the same time. "First, you must see it, Eli. Then you can make it real."

"What do you mean? How do you make it?"

He waved away my questions with one paw, his eyes squeezed shut. "No, no. Don't begin with what you don't understand. Always begin where you are, not where you aren't. Listen to me. First, you must see it. Then you can make it real."

I stared down at him, but he wasn't looking back. His eyes were pressed shut. A fierce scowl dominated his face. I looked around at the green field, the retreating storm clouds now miles away on the horizon, the sun reflecting off rain puddles all over the field.

It occurred to me that closing my eyes might help, so I did.

Nothing.

"How am I supposed to see something," I asked, "when I don't know what it looks like?"

"Wrong question. What do you want?"

I opened my eyes again and stared at him. "Huh?"

AlBaer sat in the same position, his eyes shut, one paw raised. "What do you want?"

"I want to run fast."

"Then see that in your mind. So strongly you can smell it, taste it. See it from every angle. Then, when you know not just that it *might* be, but that it *must* be, then the stuff of miracles will be at your fingertips and you only have to reach out and grab it. It will become just as you see it."

"But what if I can't see it?"

"You *can* see it, drat you!" His voice grew positively icy. "You can see anything if you really want to. Your problem is that you are seeing everything else. Close your eyes."

A chill went up my spine. How did he know my eyes were open when his were closed? "That doesn't make any sense. Besides, I've tried that already. It didn't work."

"You see the lost souls, don't you?"

"That's different. They're really there."

"*Are* they? Close your eyes."

Groaning inwardly, I closed my eyes.

"What do you want?" he whispered.

To run. I want to run fast. Like Glyn the Strong.

A picture formed in my mind. Glyn the Strong burning over the fields of the north unknown, his tail streaming behind him. When that image had formed itself into an almost tangible picture in my mind, I substituted my own face for his. I felt stupid, but it was the only thing I could think of. I may not be able to run fast, but Glyn could. So I made a half-Glyn, half-Eli.

"No," AlBaer said. "Don't see yourself. You've done too much of that."

The weirdness of his statement sent a shock through my system. How did he know what I was imagining? Something strange—call it belief—surged through me.

I wiped away the image of the Eli-Glyn and started anew with the hills and trees flying beneath me.

I imagined myself running, my paws beating the air below, my legs pumping so fast I could not even feel them. I leapt creeks, bounded over trees, skipped wildly over hills and fields.

I passed the boulders that marked the southern border of Cadrid, and at some point I felt AlBaer's paws on my back—he must have stood—and a great wind lifted me and I began to laugh, because I had never felt anything so wonderful in my life. Better than the day Father took me through the training hall of the kingsguard, better than the one time I tasted honey fresh from a comb, better even than when fire shot out from the Rock and destroyed PaTri and the priests of Kalla.

All my life, the events of my imagination had centered on me. I imagined myself doing the exploits of Glyn the Strong, and I wanted people to adore and respect me. I wanted to be Glyn the Strong, not Eli the Mundane.

But this time was different. I didn't imagine myself. Though I ran in my mind, I saw only the woods and hills and streams, the rivers and rocks and waving prairie. I saw creation stretch out like a sleeping cat below me, and I loved it. I thought about my mother, and I loved her. And it didn't matter that what I was seeing wasn't possible, or even real.

It felt so wonderful to finally be free of myself, I barely noticed the gray, fluttering stones gathered on a hillside below.

It wasn't until my paws almost touched the ground that I realized they weren't stones, but mice. The force of that realization snapped open my eyes.

AlBaer was gone.

I stood on the side of a windswept hill under a slate-colored sky.

Mice surrounded me.

"How did you get here?" one of them asked.

"What is it?" A voice said, obviously irritated—and alarmingly familiar. "What's going on?"

The first mouse stepped out of the way, and my heart sank.

I recognized his black fur and single rotting tooth from the auction. Worse, his eyes were unmistakable.

He coughed as a dark scowl twisted his face. "Twopence." His cough turned into a chuckle. "I am surprised PaTri let you live."

Chapter Thirteen

Captured

The black mouse wore an expression of superiority, as though he knew something I didn't, which was undoubtedly true.

I knew nothing at that moment except terror. AlBaer was gone. The Known Lands were gone. I stood on the side of a grassy, windswept hill in a place I'd never imagined, let alone seen, and tried to absorb the fact that my run had been real. Or, if it hadn't been real, nothing that came before it had been real either. I could have believed myself dreaming and back in the horror of PaTri's storage chamber if not for the wind that whipped my back and neck.

"Why have you followed us?"

"Followed you?" I stared in disbelief.

His gaze flicked to one of the soldiers now standing in a semicircle behind me. A large, meaty paw clamped down on my neck and forced my head to bow.

"What," he asked, "are—you—doing—here?" He spoke slowly, as though speaking to an imbecile.

"I was sent."

He must have motioned, for the mouse gripping my neck let me lift my head high enough to see his face.

"What does PaTri want now?" His eyes narrowed.

"PaTri?" I shook my head. He doesn't know PaTri is dead, I thought. The news about their priests hasn't reached them yet. I really did come all the way from Tira-Nor. "No. Not PaTri," I said. "AlBaer. The seer."

His expression changed. "Master AlBaer of Tira-Nor? Hmm. I am surprised PaTri sold you to him. You are fortunate. Is there a message?"

I thought quickly. I knew better than to lie. I never was good at lying, and AlBaer hadn't given me any message. But was there an implied message? He had sent me on a quest—a quest of my own choosing. "I am to find a certain mouse. Edina. A female slave. If she still lives. She was sent to Cadrid many seasons ago."

Something like surprise flitted across his face, then disappeared. "I will make inquiries when we arrive." He turned and motioned to the soldiers, and my audience ended. "Put him to work in my crew. See that he survives. He belongs to Master AlBaer, and I do not want to have to replace him. But that is no reason he cannot be useful."

He grunted and waddled up the long grassy slope, toward the crest of the hill.

The soldier holding my neck shoved me downhill toward a long train of burdened mice.

◆ ◆ ◆

We marched twenty hours a day for the next four days. Each day the sun mounted a little higher in a cloudless sky, gathering heat that lingered into the dark hours of early morning.

Except for Black Fur's muscular bodyguard, who carried him on a covered litter, the soldiers moved unburdened. But we were lashed in teams of four to long poles strung with seeds and dried berries from Tira-Nor, and the days were merciless. Exhaustion followed us like a great hound.

I slept on the ground and found dreamless sleep almost instantly whenever I was allowed to rest. I began to understand why many did not survive the journey.

The soldiers fed us snatches of low-grade food from the poles, and allowed us to drink whenever chance or fate brought us near water.

Perhaps I should have been grateful. Compared to the treatment the others received, my captivity was easy. I was first to be untied when we stopped to sleep, and last to be lashed to the pole in the morning. I never felt the fists of the taskmasters. And I always got more food than the others, too. Not much more. Just enough to make it obvious that I belonged in some category besides "doomed." I was borrowed property, something to be returned when Cadrid was done with me.

I learned from snatched whispers that Black Fur's name was Hammah, meaning, imaginatively, "black of fur." The Cadridians in the caravan called him Surrah Hammah, *Surrah* being the Cadridian word for Lord, Master, Superior Being, Great Pompous Muckety-Muck, Mouse Who Looks the Same Coming and Going, and, apparently, Someone Who Can Have You Killed Painfully with No Questions Asked. They carried him on a litter made of ash and decorated with carvings of talons, so that it seemed to be carried by invisible birds of prey. When Hammah spoke, the Cadridians answered quickly, with long, elaborate bows. "Yes, Surrah Hammah," they would say. Or, in the case of a negative, "Unfortunately, Surrah Hammah, the answer to your question is no, Surrah Hammah."

Hammah's position was not owing to noble blood. According to slave gossip, the king of Cadrid had appointed him royal steward as a reward for courage and leadership in battle.

Step by step we plodded on, far beyond the Known Lands—those regions the kingsguard had mapped and defended. So far that I doubted I could find my way home. If Tira-Nor could still be called home. I didn't know. Nothing made sense. Why had AlBaer sent me to be captured? Why save my life only to surrender it?

Where was my mother?

My paws blistered. The pressure of the pole rubbed my shoulders raw. Every joint ached continually. I did not complain. The condition of the others shamed me to silence. They had borne the same burden far longer than I.

On the morning of the fourth day, I helped a squad of Cadridian slaves bury two Tira-Norans. They were older mice, a husband and wife who had died sometime during the night.

I helped scrabble out a shallow hole in a briar thicket, and we rolled the bodies into it. Then we shoved some dirt over the grave and I waited for the overseer to perform the death rites.

"That's it," he said. He sniffed and wiped his snout with one paw. "Back to the caravan."

"Someone should speak over them," I said.

He sneered. "What for?"

"ElShua is watching."

"Lot of good that did 'em. Forget it." He turned and strode through the shrubs, and the others followed. I could have escaped at that point. But what then would become of my mother?

I stood there for a moment looking at the mound of dirt, trying to remember the words of the death song, but all I could think of was the long march and the utter weariness that had stolen their lives on the very same night. The only word I could remember was *rest*, probably because I needed some, and in a way I envied them. If I had said no to AlBaer, I might have found rest in The Garden Beyond.

Anyway, why should I care? What had any Tira-Noran done for me? They were not family. The only family remaining to me was ahead of me, in Cadrid. If she still lived.

I took a deep breath. "Rest," I said, too loudly for the silence of the wood. The word sounded hollow.

I turned and stumbled back to the caravan.

That evening we came to a dense wood that spilled down a hill into a river so wide the water seemed not to move at all, but to be made of flat steel that reflected the blue of the sky.

Massive buildings, no doubt built by men many generations past, huddled against the shoreline, some standing in the water. At least two of the roofs were partially caved in.

The Cadridian overseer bade us set the litters down for a moment of rest. "You may look now," he said. "Never again shall you see the wonder of Cadrid from so high a place. Unless you are cursed to make a second peehlgrimage to Teer-Anhor." He swept one paw in a broad gesture, indicating the slaves of the caravan. "The rest of you must count yourselves honored, for you shall die in the halls of Cadrid."

◆ ◆ ◆

We entered the city in a long line behind Hammah's litter.

A breeze drifted up from the river, carrying the mingled odors of algae, wet leaves, and mud. We followed a rut scooped from the earth along an ancient, unpaved road that cut through the trees and flowed into Cadrid from the west. In places the weeds grew so thick I could not see over them.

Then buildings rose on either side, enormous and ghastly against the blue sky. On the left, a row of wooden-framed structures jutted out over the river. To the right, a warehouse of cement blocks stretched south all the way to the woods at the base of the hill from which we had descended.

As a kit I had seen the Houses of Men that stand west of Tira-Nor. Even from a distance the two-story buildings had dominated the horizon. Cadrid added eeriness to its terrifying immensity. Whereas the Houses near Tira-Nor were home to living men, Cadrid had obviously been abandoned ages ago. A pall of quiet loneliness hung over the streets. Trees sprouted from several roofs, and in one place an elm, grasping for sunlight, reached through a broken window from the blackness inside.

A sense of dread and awe settled over all of us. We walked in silence, heads craning. No doubt this is what the stewards herding us forward intended. The unspoken message was clear: you are in Cadrid, and you are insignificant.

I wondered briefly what had happened to the men who built this place, but when we passed the warehouse, my curiosity vanished and I simply gaped.

A line of mice trundled up a wooden ramp from the back of the warehouse, their heads down, their movements measured and unnatural. Their bodies were thin as shadows.

Slaves.

The taskmasters pacing on either side of the line saw Surrah Hammah's litter approaching, and one of them shouted a clipped command. Immediately the line of mice fell forward, faces in the dirt, front paws outstretched. It looked almost like a dance.

The overseer standing to the side of the rutted gravel drive motioned us on. I stared down at the bony bodies pressed to the earth as we passed by and wondered, for just a moment, what they had done to deserve such a fate. I caught myself midthought. Deserve? Why must they deserve it? Did I deserve to be here?

We lumbered into the open mouth of a three-story brick building in the center of the town and down a wide, circular staircase. The warehouse slaves must have followed us, for the line grew as we trudged to a room at the end of a short hallway. Fading sunlight shone through windows on the north wall, revealing brown cardboard boxes that smelled of mildew. There were enough boxes to carpet the floor, each perhaps the size of a single family's quarters back in Tira-Nor.

Cadridian taskmasters snapped at us as we passed, directing us in bunches of fifteen or twenty into the dark boxes. I had no room to stretch out, but lay partially upright against another mouse. Someone else leaned against me, and though I felt too exhausted to care about the bad smells and the close press of other bodies, fear gripped me.

An overseer poked his head into the doorway of our sleeping box. He spoke in the breathy accent of Cadrid, stretching his simple, humorless command into two syllables: "Sahleep."

But I knew I wouldn't. It was dark in the box.

So dark I could see almost anything.

Chapter Fourteen

Glyn the Mighty

In the spring of the year of the snow plague, a Death Legion of mice from Leer beset the city. The king of Tira-Nor sent a delegation from the palace to the Lesser Families to ask for the help of Glyn the Strong. Half a dozen of the city's most important noblemice stood in the entryway of Sir Lyn's humble quarters. Their heads were bowed with the shame of asking for help from someone of his station.

"What do you want?" Sir Lyn asked.

"We will speak to your son," Yil, Earl of the House of Greens, said stiffly. "Be quick about it."

"Of course. Glyn!"

Glyn listened from the other room, but did not emerge immediately when Sir Lyn called. Instead he busied himself weaving together a long cord of braided sawgrass. The way he saw it, those pompous snoots from the palace could wait. They had kept his father waiting for some sign of respect for many years.

For some time Yil and the other nobles wrung their paws, paced the entry chambers, and threw nervous glances at Glyn's chamber hole, but none dared enter unbidden.

At last Sir Lyn peered into Glyn's chamber himself. "What are you doing, Son?" he asked.

"Weaving a riddle," Glyn said.

"But the nobles want to see you. The Earl of Greens himself has come to speak to you. Surely you heard me calling."

"Do you want me to help them, Father?"

"Them?" Sir Lyn answered. He stepped into the chamber and spoke in a low voice. "No. But I do want you to help Tira-Nor."

"All right," Glyn said. He rose and went into the entry, dragging the long braided cord of grass behind him. He looked at each of the nobles in turn. "I have a riddle for you," he said at last to Yil. "If you can answer it, I will go out and stop the mice of Leer."

The nobles looked at each other in astonishment. The earl said, "But what if we can't answer it? The mice of Leer have come with thousands of their warriors! They are outside our gates even now!"

"Gentlemice." Glyn sighed and shook his head. "It is clear you have failed already. What sort of leader begins by considering the odds against him?

"Excuse me." Glyn walked to the entryway. No one tried to stop him.

As he stepped into the tunnel, a small, nervous voice asked, "But what was the riddle?"

"I have given it to you already," Glyn said. And he walked up the ramp, past the quaking sentries, out the Shade Gate, and into the open.

The mice of Leer surrounded him quickly, but kept their distance. Perhaps by that time Glyn's reputation had reached even to their distant city. Perhaps it was the way he stood, relaxed at the crest of the slope, the cord of grass draped over one shoulder, his expression eager.

He spoke to the ring of white faces gathered around him, more than two thousand strong. "Mice of Leer," he said. "Thank you! I had thought that I would have to travel all the way to Leer in order to spank you. But here you are, presenting yourselves to me! For your thoughtfulness I will make you a gift of a riddle." Glyn inspected the claws of his left paw. "I will stop spanking you the moment you unwrap it."

The mice of Leer snarled and lunged forward together, surrounding him, like a white fist closing on a berry.

Snap!

The cord lashed out, and its saw edges sliced more than air. From the Royal Gate, kingsguard sentries saw the white mice of Leer hesitate as Glyn's voice rang out over the fields.

"Are you ready? Here it is," Glyn called. "Cold! I make myself a shawl!"

Snap! went the cord.

"I can't get up when I fall!"

Snap!

"The warmer I get, the more I sweat!"

Snap! A sound like lightning cracking the sky wide open. *Snap! Snap! Snap!*

The fist opened. White mice flew backward, fanning out in a slow circle around him.

"Till there's nothing left of me at all!"

Leerian warriors fled down the hill.

Glyn followed, his cord lashing out like the tongue of a snake. Wherever it tasted white fur, it left a streak of red.

The mice of Leer did not care that they were being herded west, away not only from Tira-Nor, but further from home.

At Dry Gully the long mass of white spilled into rock and weed, and those behind cried out in terror, pressing their comrades from behind.

Snap! Snap! Snap! Snap! Snap! Again and again the cord lashed out.

Some say the sound was not made by the whip as it lacerated air and flesh, but by Glyn himself. They say it was not a snap, but a snort. They say Glyn was laughing through his nose.

Glyn might have followed them all the way to the ends of the earth had one of them not cried out an answer as he retreated.

"Snow!" The mouse shrieked. "Snow snow snow snow snow!"

Glyn launched the mouse into the air with a final swift kick to the backside, and then stopped chasing them. But he climbed Round Top and watched until every mouse of Leer had passed beyond the borders of the Known Lands.

When he returned to the Shade Gate, the committee from the palace waited to greet him.

Snap! went his whip once more. But this time it left only a tiny cut in the paw of one noble.

"What was that for?" the earl asked, quaking and rubbing his knuckles.

"You didn't answer my riddle," Glyn said. "But the mice of Leer did."

"You didn't give us a riddle!"

Sir Lyn pushed his way through the growing crowd and took the whip out of Glyn's paws. "He certainly did. He asked you what sort of leader begins by considering the odds against him." Sir Lyn turned to his son. "Is that right?"

Glyn nodded. "And you should have answered," he said. "For it is the glory of noblemice to unravel riddles."

The Earl of the House of Greens flushed crimson. "But that was a terrible riddle," he said.

"Only because you are terrible leaders."

Chapter Fifteen

Nothings

We awoke in darkness to the shouting of taskmasters. Someone jerked my left leg, pulling me through the opening, and I tumbled into the main hall. A mouse pointed and gave me a dispassionate shove.

Darkness painted the windows black. We formed two lines, were divided into five work parties, and marched, shivering, out into the damp pre-morning air.

Our taskmaster, SimHone, a narrow-framed mouse with a snout like a hatchet, walked by my side as we stumbled down the empty street toward the river. "Best way to stay ahlive is to keep wahrm," he said. "Best way to keep wahrm is to keep moving. Best way to keep moving is to do ahs you're told and work for His Majesty's glohry."

The street ended at a large, wood-framed building that stood halfway out over the water. On the river side, a massive wheel cut slowly into the water with heavy slaps, like the tail of a beaver.

By the time we made it inside, sunlight stood on the surface of the river and washed the mill—for that's what it was—with fiery shafts of dust. Cedar planks stood in piles on either side of the room, leaving a single corridor down the middle. At the far end, closest to the wheel, a huge metal blade hung above a long platform. It turned when the wind pushed through the broken windows and whistled against its teeth.

SimHone pointed to the top plank on the stack to our right. Waves marred its long edge, as if someone had hacked into it with thousands of tiny blades. "Behold the wealth of Cadrid!" he said to me, the newest member of his crew. "Behold your duty and joy. Thees room holds the king's stores of cedar, ready for processing." He pointed again. "You are here because you have good teeth. Perfect for such a job. Be glad you are here and not on one of the other crews." He looked out the broken window at the sunrise, then back at me.

"A good mouse can make six times his weight in cedar in one day." He sniffed. "But you are not a good mouse. You are not even a bad mouse. You are nothing." He motioned to the whole group of slaves and raised his voice as he spoke. "You are all nothings! Nothings who do not deserve the honor of touching the king's cedar." He turned and faced me. "You will make twice your weight today in cedar shavings. You will not rest or eat until you have made twice your weight. Do you understand?"

No one spoke.

SimHone took this as a yes. "Good," he said. He looked back out over the water at the rising sun. "Then best you had started now."

He turned and disappeared. I followed the others up a narrow trail cut into the wall of wood and took my place next to a middle-aged mouse. He did not even glance my way before bending over his length of wood.

I had loved the smell of cedar once, but no longer. It was a constant battle of bite, chew, spit until my throat burned and the muscles in my jaw ached. My head pounded. Slowly, my pile of moist cedar shavings grew. The guards posted below paid no attention to any of us. They lounged against the far stack of lumber and drew figures in the dust of the floor.

Occasionally, I stopped to measure my progress against that of the others. I saw no way any of us could meet the quota. Twice my own weight? Sheer dreaming. Six times? Impossible! A story meant to suck away the last vestiges of our hope, if indeed any remained. I counted myself fortunate that Hammah considered me a servant of AlBaer, a temporary slave. But how could I get a message to Hammah about my "mission"?

Mother. Edina.

Did she still live? Or was all this for nothing?

The day stretched into a monotonous repetition of two actions and a single taste. Chew, spit. Chew, spit. Chew, spit. Broken only by the slapping of water under the wharf, the smell of dead fish, and the dry odor of sawdust that had somehow permeated the walls, which were now eaten away with the telltale holes of powder post beetles.

SimHone returned before sunset. He looked at our stacks of shavings and snarled. "A whole day and this is what you give me? You are less than nothings. You will not eat. You will not rest. You will work tonight. All night! I will make mice out of you!"

He stomped outside and the guards changed and the cedar-plank mice turned back to their planks. One mouse shrugged as if to say, I expected as much. It occurred to me that perhaps this was a daily ritual. Maybe they never met their quota, and SimHone's abuse was just part of the show. But there was no mistaking the look of defeat in the eyes of the other Tira-Norans. They had given up a long time ago.

They were not mice any more. They were slaves.

"No," I said.

A guard at the base of the stack cocked his head to one side and said something to the others I didn't understand.

"No," I said, louder than before. I turned and sat with my legs hanging over the edge of the plank and glared down at him. The slaves cast furtive glances at me and attacked their boards with renewed vigor, as if to distance themselves from my rebellion.

He scowled and spoke to two others, who disappeared down either end of the corridor. A flanking maneuver. The guard narrowed his eyes and climbed with deliberation. He knew what he was doing. The way he moved—the short steps, the pauses, the sideways glances—all told me he knew exactly how long it would take for his goons to show up on my left and right.

I had a temporary height advantage, but would have to take a beating from all three of them if I stayed put. I stood and shifted to my right, so I could look straight down from above him as he climbed. "I demand to be taken to Surrah Hammah," I said. "I am the servant of AlBaer, seer of Tira-Nor and advisor to King Ahaz." This was a bit of a stretch, but AlBaer had given the king advice, so it wasn't an outright lie. Besides, I doubted the big gloomy thug below me understood anything I said.

He stopped anyway and looked up, shifty-eyed. I could tell he was trying not to look to either side and thus give away the ambush.

"AlBaer," I repeated. "Of Tira-Nor. I am on a mission. I have been sent to look for a mouse named Edina. Why am I being treated as a common slave?"

The guard below me lowered his head and started climbing again. I could tell it was some sort of signal, so I didn't wait. I launched myself off the plank and hit him in the shoulders with both feet. The other two guards must have been close by; one of them swore.

Gloomy pitched backward off the pile and landed on his back beneath me. I didn't look to see if he was hurt. I hit the ground in a spray of cedar shavings and dust, rolled to the far pile, and launched myself toward the open doors at the far end of the hall.

Wrong direction. A line of Cadridian soldiers waited in the corridor, as though they were expecting me. SimHone stood behind them, scowling wickedly, his fur yellow in a shaft of orange sunlight from the window.

I turned and fled the opposite way.

Lying on his back, Gloomy shook his head. I kicked him in the face as I ran by and sprinted through a jagged hole in the far door and out onto the wharf.

It was a dead end.

The wharf stuck out over the water like a tongue. Its warped slats ran diagonally into posts of gray deadwood that supported a sagging safety rail. Beyond, the river swirled in a slow current of mysterious blues and browns.

Guards shot through the hole in the door and spread out in a line across the wharf.

I jumped onto the lowest railing and stuck my head out over the water. Perhaps I could climb down onto one of the crossbeams.

Impossible. The wood was slick with oil and moisture. It was either face my captors or plunge into the river.

"I am a servant of AlBaer," I said. "Seer of Ahaz, king of Tira-Nor, and voice of ElShua in the Known Lands. I am neither your servant nor your slave. I am on a mission to find the female mouse Edina, and I demand to be taken to her immediately."

SimHone stepped through, then Gloomy, who plodded onto the creaking timber holding his jaw and looking as though he wanted to see blood.

"If you come quietly, I will ask Surrah Hammah for leniency," SimHone said. "You will not get another chance."

Gloomy gave him a bitter sideways glance and clenched one paw into a fist.

"Who are you to offer me a second chance?" I said, furious. "I am not yours to command."

SimHone brushed the objection aside with the wave of one paw. "You are a servant of His Majes—"

"I am *not*!" I shouted. "I do not belong to Cadrid." The guards stopped, though they were nearly close enough to reach out and grab me.

Gloomy stepped forward, but SimHone stuck out one arm and held him back. "You use the name of AlBaer lightly. Nor do you call yourself by ElShua, the god of Tira-Nhor. Why should we account AlBaer's honor to you?"

He waited a long moment for my answer, but I could think of nothing to convince him. At last he lowered his arm and Gloomy approached, his eyes full of controlled rage.

Holding on to the railing with one paw, I leaned out over the water and looked down into the current. Streaks of oil oozed through the shadows of the railing on the surface.

The guards edged closer. Gloomy pointed at the wheel turning downriver beside the wharf. Its jagged wooden palms slapped the water rhythmically, a slow drum beating a death march.

"Kalla," Gloomy whispered. The Cadridians seemed to think Kalla lived in this river. I wondered why Gloomy didn't reach out and grab me, then realized he wanted me in the water. "Kalla will have you, no?"

He smiled at last, perhaps for the first time ever. If Kalla were waiting for me below—

I looked at SimHone and stuck out my chest.

"No," I said.

And let go.

Chapter Sixteen

The Wheel

I came up sputtering under the wharf, just in time to catch a snout full of pier. I reached for the massive trunk of wood as the current dragged me past, but its surface was coated in oil.

The river surprised me. From above, it seemed to barely move.

I kicked out against the water and reached for the next pier, but it slid past, unsympathetic.

The wheel slapped the river. Its frame shivered under the strain; its rusting, ungreased axle was loud even against the background roar of falling water.

Whump! *Creak*. *Whump*! *Creak*. Louder and louder as the current tugged me beyond the last pier. Their eyes dispassionate, their paws draped over the gray wood as though exhausted by despair, mice lined the lowest railing above.

I flailed in the water and reached for the corner frame of the mill. My head went under with the effort. For a second, no more, I felt the wood under the water, slick with algae. Then my head came up and I saw a flat, ragged blade, dripping and green, descending like the Great Owl. I drew a shallow breath before it crashed into my outstretched arm, face, and chest, dragging me under and through the water.

Bubbles burst around my face and flew sideways over my shoulder. A muffled sound of scraping, deep as laughter, rose from the heart of the mill. For a moment I saw faces in the brown and black depths: a white shadow with a gaping mouth; Surrah Hammah, his eyes open, his expression lifeless; Father, one paw held across his eyes.

Then the wheel lifted me clear.

Cold air struck me in the face. I spat out the water in my mouth, clinging to the wooden blade as I rose higher and higher. Far below me, the river emptied over a cliff and into a jumble of rocks, shattering into little white pieces and reforming on the far side. If I let go of the blade and jumped downriver, the current would toss me over the edge.

I was trapped.

Then the blade began to turn over and, too late, I understood what was happening. The wheel was carrying me back to the upriver side of the mill.

I grabbed the edge with both paws, saw the roof of the mill checkered in gray and black shingles, and hoisted myself over as the world turned upside down.

On the wharf a mouse pointed. I considered jumping, but rejected the idea. The current would only drag me back under the mill, and I already felt exhausted.

Too quickly the arms of the wheel plunged me into the cold, wet darkness. I held my breath, forced myself to relax and cling to the blade, knowing the wheel would lift me up again. For one bad moment the wheel seemed to stop, and I thought, *This is where I die*, and then the air hit me for the second time.

I clung to the blade, weary and freezing, knowing I would never make it through the water a third time. I waited until the lip of the blade rose above treetops on the horizon, out of sight of the wharf, and jumped from the wheel to the roof. I meant to leap further, but my legs refused.

I fell, hit the wood shingles on all fours, and slid slowly down the roof. Even my claws could get no traction. I landed in a battered, rusting gutter filled nearly to the brim with rotting leaves.

Another foul odor. As if Cadrid might hold anything else.

I took stock of myself, too tired to marvel that I had no broken bones, too tired even to worry that my aching body could be seen from the sky.

Despite the horrible stench and the emptiness of my stomach—or perhaps because of them—I passed out.

Chapter Seventeen

War

I forced myself upright at morning light and squished through muck toward the downspout. Every muscle ached. I stank of the river and my mouth still tasted like a chunk of dry cedar. I needed clean water and food. My mother, if she still lived, might be anywhere. My survival depended on hiding from SimHone and the other Cadridians. My mission demanded the opposite. How was I to find my mother—much less free her—without their help?

I thought of AlBaer. He was probably eating raisins in RuHoff's cave right about now. Or still sleeping on a cozy little pallet. I said a short, silent prayer that he might choke on his breakfast, then risked a look over the side of the gutter.

For a long time I stood there staring, even though the sun was so bright on the water I had to blink away tears. Light rippled on the surface and caught the spray rising from the waterfall. Diamonds shivered and dripped from the blades of the wheel. The trees on the far bank looked like black and green clouds floating above the earth.

Below me, stones plunged into a lapping tongue of water. I could not see the wharf because the gutter ran along the wrong slope of the roof, but the shore down-river spread out beneath me in jumbles of silver-white water and rocks black with moisture.

I thought, *Cadrid is beautiful.*

And hated myself for thinking it.

I smelled the Cadridian soldiers before I heard them. The scent of their oil-heavy, unwashed fur emerged above the stench of the river and of rotting gutter sludge. I turned to my right and looked down into the street, where clusters of soldiers gathered in the shadows of buildings.

I ducked behind the lip of the gutter and moved north, closer to the wheel. The roof was not too steep to climb once the sun burned away the morning dew. I bounded down the far side in the shadow of the tar paper valley. A short elbow of guttering hung from the corner where the two sections met. I dropped into it and watched. Mice formed up into companies and bat-talions, then left in small groups, disappearing down the single rut by which we had come two days earlier.

I wondered what I was seeing. An evacuation? A military exercise?

A litter appeared, winding north up the street, carried on the shoulders of eight burly mice. They lowered the ash poles to the ground on the opposite side of the street, and a black shape swung off the platform.

Hammah. I recognized the arrogant way he stood.

The warriors closest to him formed a square, half in shadow and half bathed in sunlight.

He spoke loudly, his voice rising in the still, cool air of the morning. "Soldiers," he said, then lifted one paw to his mouth, coughing. "You go with shame. You must return with honor."

"Surrah!" someone shouted, then the rest of them: "Surrah! Surrah! Surrah!"

Hammah stepped aside to let the company move off. The mice at the edges of the formation struggled through the tall grass bordering the rut.

When the last company passed out of sight, two of Hammah's guards hefted the ash pole. He seemed to fold in on himself as he leaned against the pole, head lowered. His shoulders shook with a fit of coughing. His bodyguard looked away.

I ran to the end of the gutter and stuck my head into the downspout. It stank, but a thin barb of sunlight browned the blackness at the bottom. I dropped into it, but fell only a short distance. I had to burrow my way through to the bottom.

By the time I came out onto the street, Hammah was already back inside the litter and the guards were hoisting it skyward.

I ran south and planted myself in their path. "Surrah Hammah," I shouted. "What has my master done to deserve this dishonor?" I bowed low, my gaze sweeping the litter. I dared not look at Hammah's face, but forced myself to look down even when I heard the guards approach, as though Father's paw were once again shoving my head downward.

The litter creaked as Hammah lifted his bulk out of it to tower over me. His shadow draped my face. Another fit of coughing. After a long silence, one black paw lifted my chin. Still I kept my eyes lowered.

"Twopence," Hammah said. "You did not die."

"I am the servant of AlBaer, Surrah Hammah. On a mission of peace in his name. Why have you dishonored Master AlBaer?" Since they seemed to respect the old seer I figured it couldn't hurt to drop his name as many times as possible. "By refusing his request to take me to the female slave, Edina?"

I risked a look upward.

Hammah stroked his chin, his eyes narrowed almost to slits. "You talk of peace and honor. But this very day has Cadrid sent half our warriors to an uncertain fate. We go to war, not peace. Because of our shame. Brought about by the treachery of Tira-Nor. You are fortunate to be alive."

"Fortunate, Surrah Hammah? Would you consider yourself fortunate to be alive if it meant you had to tell your king that you had failed an assigned mission?"

One of the guards scowled and moved toward me, but Hammah waved him away.

"I have no obligation, Twopence. What will you give in exchange for this slave, this Edina?"

"Exchange?" Was he offering me an opportunity to free my mother?

"Why should I help you?" he asked. "What will you do for me?"

My mind slammed shut. I could think of nothing he might want, nothing I possessed which I might offer. Yet an idea seemed to form on my lips. I said the words without thinking. "I will give you myself, Surrah Hammah. I am young and fit. Surely I am more valuable than one aging female."

He offered a thin smile. "You offer what you do not have."

"Surrah?"

"You belong to AlBaer, seer of King Ahaz of Tira-Nor, and voice of ElShua in the Known Lands, do you not?"

I looked down again, angry with myself for this misstep.

"However, you do have something of value to me. Give me what I want, and I will have you taken to this Edina. This slave mouse who makes my meals, and who is also your mother."

For a moment I did nothing but stare, my jaw hanging down. At last I said, "Anything, Hammah."

"Tell me about Tira-Nor's defenses."

A fist clutched at my chest. "Surrah?"

"How many guards watch the gate holes? How strong is the kingsguard? How do the renowned wall-stones work? Where are the false passages and hidden snares?"

"I—"

He stooped down and fixed my eyes with a gaze as fierce as a jackal's. "They wanted to burn you alive, Twopence. Do not look shocked that I know of this. I know much about you and your master. I know about the death of my priests. I know what AlBaer has done.

And now I will find out what you will do. Tell me about the wall-stones."

In one sense, Hammah was right. PaTri had tried to burn me alive. They had chanted the death song over me as I passed by, had planned a picnic around my torture. So I didn't think of what Hammah wanted as treason. And yet the thought of speaking made my stomach turn. Did I owe Tira-Nor anything? Or was this an opportunity? A chance to pay back those who had hurt me with a revenge so terrible it might never be forgotten?

I would have told him everything if it weren't for the whisper that crept into my soul. My father's voice spinning back to the present from the distant shores of the past. *"When we stop saying no,"* Father said in a voice as soft as ice melting, *"they will stop feeling the need to ask. And then there will be no free mice left in Tira-Nor. The Commons will be enslaved."*

I closed my eyes. I'm sorry, Mother!

"Surrah Hammah," I said, looking up. "You ask for something I cannot give you."

Hammah let out a long, disapproving breath and motioned to the guards.

Chapter Eighteen

The Love of Glyn

Glyn the Strong traveled widely across the Known Lands. He even went beyond the realm of Tira-Nor, coming and going at the slightest whim. Sometimes he stayed away for weeks, and other times he reappeared after a few hours with stories of distant lands no one had ever heard of.

Sir Lyn and Lady Gredda put their son's behavior down to youth and a wild nature. He had no real friends. Who could be expected to befriend a freak of nature? What might anyone have in common with a mouse feared by predators as fierce as the eagle and the fox? The most outrageous activities of his peers dulled in comparison to the things he did every day without even thinking. Besides, none of them liked riddles.

So when Glyn came home one day and announced his intention to marry a young mouse from Leer, his parents were unsure how to respond. He needed a friend. But a girl from Leer? Was he really ready to marry?

"There may be . . ." Lady Gredda said hesitantly.

"Problems," Sir Lyn added.

"Problems in such a marriage." Lady Gredda clasped her paws together so tightly her knuckles turned white. "No matter how . . . how wonderful she is . . ."

"You must consider, Son . . ."

"You must consider whether the two of you . . . that is to say . . ."

"How do you know if . . ." Sir Lyn began.

"What if the two of you are not suited for each other?" Lady Gredda bit her lower lip.

"I thought," Glyn said, frowning, "that you would be pleased."

"We are pleased," Sir Lyn said. "And if you were an ordinary mouse, this would perhaps not present such a problem. But Leer will not have forgiven you for thrashing them at the Shade Gate. Will this girl—"

"Dawna."

"Dawna. Will this girl, Dawna, adopt the customs of Tira-Nor, or will she expect you to become part of her clan?"

Glyn laughed. "Me? A mouse of Leer? That could never happen!"

"She may think differently," Gredda said.

Glyn thought for a long time. "I have been denied many things," he finally said. "I have no friends because everyone fears me. I have no station because the king will not allow me to serve unless some great enemy appears at our doorstep. I cannot even eat raisins, nor tell anyone why I must leave during the feasts of the Great Hall. And I do not complain. Surely, this one thing is not too much to ask."

Lady Gredda sighed. "Are you sure you're seeing this situation clearly?"

"Are you sure," Sir Lyn asked, "that this isn't a trap?"

"A trap!" Glyn said. "For me? I'm Glyn the Strong!"

Sir Lyn and Lady Gredda looked at each other, and then nodded. "If you will love her," Sir Lyn said, "then so will we."

Glyn did not even stop to eat dinner, but left that evening and ran through the Dark Forest and past the world beyond to the rolling country of Leer.

He arrived at an old, weathered barn the color of rusting tin and announced himself to the white-furred sentries, who led him before the girl's father.

"A mouse of Nor?" the old mouse said. He gathered a huge wad of saliva into one cheek and spat it out in front of Glyn. "Bah! I'll give you my daughter the day you bring me the whiskers of a dozen mortal enemies! Now get out of here before I throw you out."

Glyn made no response. He left the barn and ran all the way back through the realms of the east until he came to the Dark Forest, and then raced through shadow and brush to the fields of Tira-Nor. But he didn't stop at Tira-Nor. Instead, he kept running all the way to the Houses of Men.

Dusk was falling when he arrived at the place of trash and found his first mortal enemy. The orange tomcat was famous for haunting the dark openings and sagging cardboard of the dump. Local mice called him Stripe because of the faint black edges on the fur along his back. Many mice had died under his claws, though none quickly.

His tail twitched when Glyn approached. His green eyes narrowed. His chest lowered. He did not wait for Glyn to reach a perfect place of vulnerability, but struck in a blur of confident motion. He did not know it was Glyn the Strong he attacked.

Glyn caught the weight of Stripe's attack in one paw and heaved the cat over onto his back. He grabbed him by the left ear and hauled his face down to earth. "You're wasting my time," Glyn said. And he plucked a single whisker from his cheek.

"Excuse me," Stripe said. "I didn't recognize you. Are you going to kill me?"

"Are you going to kill me, *sir*!"

"Are you going to kill me, sir?" Stripe repeated.

"Not today," Glyn said, letting go.

The next evening he returned to Leer and set twelve whiskers—each from a different cat—before Dawna's father.

The old mouse's eyes popped.

"I have come for your daughter," Glyn said. "According to your terms. Twelve mortal enemies."

"What are those?" Her father pointed.

"Cat whiskers," Glyn said.

But if Dawna's father was impressed, he showed no signs of it. Instead, his face burned red. He looked around at the small crowd of Leerians who had gathered to stare at the sheaf of white whiskers, stiff as pine needles on the dirt floor. "Who can kill one cat and live?" he asked.

"You said nothing of killing," Glyn replied. "You only asked for their whiskers."

Dawna's nine brothers scowled and murmured under their breath.

"Aha," the old mouse said. "This knave has tried to steal my daughter by deception. Throw him out!"

"Knave?" Glyn replied. "Deception?" He pointed to the crowd of Leerians in a broad, sweeping motion. "For that I will punish all of you."

◆ ◆ ◆

The return journey to Tira-Nor took longer than Glyn had anticipated. He had not expected Dawna to walk so slowly, and her smile, which had previously warmed his heart, did not travel with them.

Sir Lyn and Lady Gredda welcomed the young Leerian into their home, but she rarely spoke, and it was clear she was unhappy.

"She doesn't love you, Son," Lady Gredda told him.

"She'll get over it," Glyn said.

But after two weeks, little had changed except Glyn's mood. He had expected marriage to bring him happiness, friendship, and love. Instead, every day brought a new humiliation, a new rejection. He had no more friends now than before.

"Did you really beat her father?" Sir Lyn asked one day.

Glyn nodded.

"And her brothers?"

Again, Glyn nodded.

"You promised to love her," Sir Lyn said. "Was that love?"

"He set the price!" Glyn said, pounding the floor with one fist so hard the walls shook. "And I paid it!"

Sir Lyn sighed. "Did you really pay what he asked?"

"Twelve cats. I plucked their whiskers with one paw. Each of them called me sir."

"I'm sure that isn't what Dawna's father meant," Sir Lyn said. "He wasn't asking for proof that you were a brute. He was asking you to prove that you love her."

"How better to prove my love," Glyn asked, "than to face twelve cats in a single day?"

"Were you an ordinary mouse, I might agree."

"So because I am strong, I must pay more? Do more? Give more?"

"Yes!" Sir Lyn said. "Your strength isn't for you. It's for everyone else."

Glyn rose and stalked to the entryway. "I can see it is time for me to move out. Dawna and I will go to RuHoff's cave."

Chapter Nineteen

The Warehouse

I slept in a different crate that night, jammed into a pile of exhausted slaves who slept without moving. Hours before dawn a team of taskmasters kicked and prodded us awake, then shoved us outside and down a long ramp.

We formed into a ragged square and stood unmoving as a thick mouse with darting eyes counted us. My stomach turned as I stole glances at the mice around me. Moonlight revealed what I could not see in the darkness of the crate: fur hung from their bones in papery sheets. They neither spoke nor moved, except to shiver in the cold night air.

"What are we doing?" I whispered to the mouse on my right, a tall mouse with sunken eyes and a nose like a dorsal fin.

My words struck him like a physical blow. He blinked and turned his head slightly, then closed his eyes.

"What are we doing?" I asked again, this time a little louder.

Fish-face squinted lines into his cheeks and shook his head in short, quick denials.

The mouse in front of him scowled at me over one shoulder.

A taskmaster's head appeared above the crowd. "Who's talking?" he snarled.

Silence.

"Who?!"

No one moved. The taskmaster fixed his gaze on a short gray-hair two steps in front of me. "You've been here long enough to know better," he said, and brought one fist down into his victim's snout.

When he pulled his arm back for another blow I stepped forward. "Me," I said. "It was me. First day."

The taskmaster paused for only a moment. He struck the mouse again, harder this time, and delivered a punishing kick to his midsection. The mouse made no effort to resist. He lay on the wood and groaned softly.

The taskmaster sidled up to me. "You're him," he said.

"Eli, son of—"

He struck me then, not just once, but dozens of times. It would not have been so bad had I not struck back, but when the other taskmasters saw him go down, they descended on me like wasps and took turns pummeling my face and stomach. After a while I gave in. Not because I would not resist, but because I could not. My face exploded with pain. Something in my gut shifted at one of their blows, and the agony was like that of the thorn in my paw, but without the softening delirium. It pulsed between my ribs and my nose, and my arms and legs betrayed me.

Eventually, the other taskmasters left me lying on the quay and retreated to the edge of the group. The first taskmaster lowered himself to look me in the eye. "You want to leave this place? Go ahead. Swim for it." He pointed across the river to the far bank, where a black line of trees lay mashed under the horizon, barely visible in the moonlight. "But if you don't make it to the other side, I'll kill you myself."

Even Glyn the Strong would not have dared that journey, and I couldn't move without pain.

The taskmaster stood, raised one fist in the air, and pointed to the water with the other paw. "Kalla will have you in the end." He turned in a slow circle. "All of you."

The others did not even look at him. They stared out over the river with that same blank expression.

Kalla? The river? I didn't understand what he meant. *Kalla isn't a river*, I thought. *She's an ugly dark lizard with greenish-white lips.*

Silence returned, except for the lapping of the black water below the quay. The other slaves stood unmoving, as quiet and unperturbed as stones. I lay very still and watched through one eye as blood flowed from my nose and mouth, pooled on the weathered boards, and dripped into a crack toward the shifting, black shadows. Beneath me, shapes moved in the darkness and nibbled at my blood.

When the sun finally rose, I raised my head and caught my first glimpse of the back of the warehouse. The river below the falls ran hard against a line of low wooden quays that jutted over the water like the blade of a long saw. Behind us, opening on the old quay, an ugly brick building backed against the shore of the river.

Apparently, I had seen Cadrid at its best. That is, I had seen Cadrid from a distance. Now I would see it as a flea sees one's skin.

Fist pointed at Fish-face and another mouse. "Help him into the warehouse. He'll work like the rest of you."

Mice hooked me by the armpits and drew me upright. Blood pounded behind my forehead. The world teetered, but I shrugged off the helping paws and staggered across the quay and through the dark doors of the warehouse behind the others.

Inside, morning light slanted through high windows and mixed dust with air in a sort of dizzying dance. Steel shelves the color of old milk lined the walls, and on the shelves stood row upon row of sagging, greasy cardboard boxes.

Dust swirled into the air around us, kicked up by our paws as we wound past piles of debris: metal rods, rotting boards with exposed nails, a split rubber tube, plastic bins and buckets, and strips of dirty cloth.

In the corner, we shimmied up a steel leg and huddled together behind a cardboard box on the top shelf. I lagged behind, my aching limbs rebelling at the effort of the climb. When I reached the top there was no room on the open front side of the shelf. We stood jammed together between the box and the wall, noses twitching. Peanut. That's what it was. The place reeked of peanut butter.

I peered over the edge at the concrete floor below. Taskmasters glared up at me. "New day," one of them shouted. "New delivery. Best get the opening over with early, before you're all tired and kill someone. Grease!"

A thin, haggard-looking old mouse stuck his face around the corner of the box and looked down. "Surrah?"

"Pick your wedge and shoulder."

Grease turned and scanned the mice in our group. For an instant I thought he would pick me, but the swelling of my face must have dissuaded him. "You and you." He pointed behind me.

Two mice exchanged resolute glances and heaved themselves up to the top of the cardboard box beside us. One by one we clambered up after them.

Someone had already chewed a hole across the front and top of the box. We positioned ourselves around the dark blue ridges of the plastic lid that was just visible below us, in the shadows of the box.

Grease motioned to a long, lean mouse. "You first, Skinny."

Skinny didn't protest. He took a deep breath and bounded from the top of the box to the lid, then lowered himself between the outermost jar and the one behind him, the one directly under the cardboard we stood on. He gripped the lid with his forepaws and shoved with his hind legs.

Skinny closed his eyes and puffed, his cheeks making soft popping sounds with the effort. Slowly, the edge of the jar lifted. The black line of space around the lid began to widen.

"Serious," Grease said. "Shoulder."

Serious dropped to a seated position behind Skinny, placing his legs across Skinny's shoulders, and shoved against the lid.

Grease stared at the opening. "Get ready," he said.

The jar creaked as it lifted, tipping slowly upward and forward over open space, into the morning sunlight.

"Now!"

Mice dropped into the gap. First three, then four, then six.

Grease motioned to me. "Now you."

I slipped into the gap between Skinny and Fishface and did what everyone else was doing. I pushed, sliding awkwardly down the further the jar leaned forward. As the jar rose, the lid moved away from the lip of the cardboard box we clung to. Our legs stretched out, and we had to hunch down in the gap and cling to the box with our forepaws. Soon my paws cramped and sweat poured off me in streams.

I glanced sideways. Skinny's face was swollen with effort. His eyes bulged and his head craned forward on a neck that seemed half again too long. But the taskmasters were too far away to hear us speak, so I said, "I'm looking . . . for a mouse."

Skinny ignored me. My legs began to shake. The jar seemed to grow heavier as the edge lifted.

"Her name is Edina," I said. "Probably works . . . in the kitchen."

He shook his head. "Shut," he said, "your face."

I felt as though more than just the jar was tipping over. If another slave—a mouse of Tira-Nor—wouldn't even speak to me, I had no hope of finding my mother. "Please!" I said. "They can't hear us."

All at once the jar reached its apex and didn't move at all. It hung there, suspended half on, and half off the shelf. Skinny turned to look at me, his eyes as empty as old nutshells.

Without warning, the other mice scrabbled back to the top of the box. From the floor below, the voices of taskmasters suddenly erupted in a confused, meaningless explosion of orders.

Skinny just stayed there, legs stretched out so far he was almost horizontal. He looked almost confused, as though he were about to go to sleep. Then, as the jar tipped forward, he let go of the box edge.

I reached out. Grabbed frantically for his arm.

Missed.

I lost my grip on the box as the jar plunged over the steel horizon. I would have fallen with it, but other paws grabbed me and hauled me backward to safety.

A series of sharp cracks split the air as the jar hit concrete and bounced. The taskmasters stopped yelling all at once. Underneath those sounds, a dull thud, thick with meaning and heavier than the silence that followed it, filled the shadows.

"Where is he?" I asked. But I already knew the answer.

I looked up at Grease. He stood motionless, staring. They were all staring, all of the slaves, staring wide-eyed and silent at the empty space beyond the metal edge of the shelf.

◆ ◆ ◆

The taskmasters tapped me for the burial, along with Fish-face, Stubs, and a short, scrawny mouse everyone called Serious. We hauled Skinny's body out onto the quay and placed it under the railing.

"On three," Grease said. He seemed unconcerned about being overheard. Apparently, the taskmasters had no intention of involving themselves in the death rites.

"Shouldn't someone say something?" I asked.

Grease turned and gave me a puzzled look. At last he shrugged. "If you want to, go ahead."

But no words would come. I had never seen a funeral. Not a real one. Just the burial of the old mouse and his wife in the forest between Tira-Nor and Cadrid. And anyway, what did it matter? What good did words do when Skinny was dead?

Serious seemed to guess what I was thinking. "One way or another," he whispered in a far-off voice, "Kalla will have us. He's never denied."

"Kalla?" I asked. "They believe she lives here, don't they?"

"She?" Grease nodded to the water. "Name of the river. Kalla. And their god. The god and the river are . . ." He shrugged as though searching for the right words to explain a difficult concept, ". . . the same. One thing but . . . different forms." He reached down and grabbed one of Skinny's ankles. "We have to do it now. They're watching."

I took one wrist and we lifted, swung twice, and on the third pass heaved Skinny's body out over the waves.

When the sun set we were herded back up the ramp, through the street, and down the dark staircase to our tiny crate. I was exhausted, but sleep eluded me.

The darkness of the sleeping chamber was absolute.

And so, of course, I could see.

◆ ◆ ◆

In the realm of flesh, Kalla flowed with oil and reed. She vomited dead fish and bleached leafless wood onto her shores. She lapped at the piers of the city like a thirsting animal. In the world of the not-flesh, the world of thoughts and dreams and fears, Kalla walked on solid earth in a shapeless, black body. The Cadridians did not think of her as a lizard but as an unformed darkness that flooded any place without light. They thought of her as a creeping god of inevitability, the slow licking away of one's mind and will, the short or long disintegration of every mouse's soul into nothingness. They did not think of Kalla as two separate things: a river and a nothingness. The two were connected. The river was darkness, and darkness was the river. Life had come from water and would go back to it. Life had come from nothing and would go back to nothing. Life was meaningless, the river was meaningless, darkness was meaningless. Life, like light, was a temporary state, an interruption in the natural chaos of the world, to be snuffed out like a candle flickering in a random rain.

Kalla was Kalla.

◆ ◆ ◆

Time passed, but only at the edges. Days dragged into weeks, growing longer and hotter as the summer fattened itself and made our suffering more intense. Longer days meant more light by which to work, more heat to sap our strength.

I felt some part of myself slipping away, as though I had no real identity, as though my soul were washing away into the river. Each day differed from every other only by the bits of weather we experienced going to and from the warehouse. Each night we crept back down the basement steps and fell in—a jumble of exhausted bodies in a single, guarded sleeping crate.

I fingered the puzzle of my existence constantly at first. Why had I come here? Where was my mother? Why had AlBaer let me be captured? Why did I not just give in and tell Hammah what he wanted to know?

After a while, these questions blurred in my mind. *Why* slowly faded to *what*. Not *what* is life about, but *what* must be moved *where*?

Weariness turned into despair.

I felt more alone than ever, though I moved in a haze of activity, surrounded by mice who should have been—and possibly were—my brothers.

Each day it took a greater act of will to remind myself who I was and what I needed to do. On the shelf, when the taskmasters below turned away, I would maneuver myself next to someone unfamiliar and whisper questions into his ear.

"Have you heard of a mouse named Edina?" I would ask.

"No."

It was always no. Sometimes they answered before I even finished the question. "She's a slave," I would say. "From Tira-Nor. Probably looks like me."

"Quit yapping or they'll notice."

"But they aren't looking," I would say.

"No."

"Probably works in the palace."

"No."

"Cooking or—"

"I don't know her, I tell you!"

And eventually I knew what the answer would be before I asked the question, and yet didn't care that the answer was going to be no.

It didn't happen at once. It was a slow drip, a melting away of my self. But I knew one morning that I had ceased to be a Tira-Noran, ceased to be a seer's apprentice, ceased even to be a son. I knew that I would never find anyone who had seen my mother because PaTri had been right.

Edina was dead.

That was why everyone said no. They hadn't seen her because no one had seen her in years. Her body had been thrown into the river many seasons ago, before I came to Cadrid, before Father was killed, before King Ahaz and Queen IsaBel began plotting to steal our chambers back in Tira-Nor.

We were standing in rows in the predawn darkness, soaked to the bones. Warm rain pattered on the boards of the quay as we waited for sunrise. Clouds shrouded the moon, turning the water and the warehouse and the line of docks into three smudges of black.

Such mornings were a relief, for the taskmasters huddled under cover of the overhang, and the sound of the rain made whispered conversations possible, if rare.

I stood behind a newbie. He had a black snout with wire-brush whiskers and short, black hair. His pudgy belly told me he was a reject from the upper classes. *Must have done something terrible to be sentenced to death's door*, I thought. And then, *He won't last long.*

He kept looking around, as though expecting someone to tell him this was all a big mistake, that he of all people need not stand out here in the rain. Tension knotted his shoulders, dripped off his fur with every quirky movement and jerk of his head. I would not have paid any attention to him were it not for a white birthmark that showed through his dripping fur at the base of his neck.

Father had carried a similar mark. And though I cared nothing for this new mouse, he held my attention.

I knew by watching him that he was working up the courage to plead his case to the taskmasters. I could see it as clearly as if it had already happened. He would shake his shoulders and straighten his back, then saunter over to Fist and his pals with a walk that was both over- and under-practiced, and ask to speak to whoever was in authority. And Fist would play along for a minute because this was something he had never seen before—or perhaps had seen a dozen times before, and liked the way it always ended. And Newbie would pull out a name Fist would recognize, try to impress the taskmasters with his connections, his lineage, his options.

Fist would shake his head knowingly, attentively, and stroke his chin with one stubby finger, and let the silence stretch into a long moment of terror. I could see it in the dark playing out, though my eyes saw only the black ink of the night.

And then Fist would kill him. He would club Newbie again and again, and when he was finished he would dump the body in the river. And at some point, either in the clubbing or the dragging, Fist would lay his foul hands on my father's birthmark, and father would die all over again.

In front of me, Newbie shook his shoulders. Straightened his back. Cleared his throat.

I stepped forward and grabbed the fur on his back, stuck my snout in his ear. "Don't do it," I whispered. "They'll kill you."

He turned and looked into my face, an expression of bewilderment painting his face even in the darkness. I could see his thought written on his face: *How does he know?*

But I didn't care what he thought. I didn't even know why I wanted to stop him. Not really. He wasn't my father. He wasn't even a Tira-Noran. He was a Cadridian. Upper class. Probably bought and sold slaves himself. Besides which, I knew by looking at his soft paws and flabby belly that he didn't have long to live.

It was something Father would have done, I decided. But even that thought didn't strike me as important. Father? Who was Father? Who was Mother? Everyone important was dead.

And yet I decided to ask him the question, because it was all I had left. I knew what the answer would be, but I asked anyway. The day I stopped asking the question would be the day I died.

I glanced toward the warehouse, saw the huddled mass of shadow-bodies under cover, and pressed my snout next to his ear. "Have you seen a mouse named Edina?" I asked. My voice sounded sterile, as cold and thin as copper wire. "She'd be old now. Probably works in the palace."

He turned again to look at me, his eyes wide.

But I already knew the answer.

I let go of him, stepped back, and settled myself into the quiet of the moment as rain dribbled through my fur and streamed down my skin.

"Edina?" he said. "Yes. Yes, of course I know her. Everyone at court knows who she is."

Chapter Twenty

Death's Door

I tried all day to steal a moment alone with Newbie to ask him where my mother was being held. It had to be in or near the palace, but I couldn't very well break into every room and expect to escape unnoticed. I needed a specific location. But the taskmasters were in a foul mood, and no opportunity presented itself until after just before sunset.

We were exhausted. Four jars in one afternoon, and working on a fifth. My legs knotted with fatigue. The taskmasters should have known something bad would happen. Perhaps they knew and didn't care.

Grease picked Newbie for wedge mouse on the fifth jar. When the gap widened far enough, Newbie dropped into the black space and started to shove.

At that moment two mice on the right lost their grip. Sweaty palms, fatigue, bad luck. Who knew the reason? A third mouse let go and sprang back, probably from fear, and that halted the jar's forward momentum.

My own fingers were locked under the blue lip of the screw-tight lid. The jar's immense weight tugged my wrists down as it slowly began to tip back into place.

Newbie saw what was happening too late. Nothing dramatic, just a slow, eye-popping squeeze during which he would not be able to breathe. It was up to the rest of us to tip the jar forward before he suffocated.

Newbie had wedged himself into the gap just to my right. His eyes widened in a silent plea for help as he shoved against the weight of the jar.

He looked at me, and I recognized the fear there. An hour ago—a moment perhaps—and his life had been blind despair and hopelessness. Now he clung to every moment as though each were meaningful.

His face purpled under the strain.

Taskmasters shouted up at us.

Infuriatingly, the two mice who had lost their grip stood there watching.

I ripped my fingers from the lid and dropped into the gap next to him, felt rather than saw his gratitude, and shoved at the jar with both legs. For a moment I slowed the crushing weight.

But I was too late.

Newbie's legs trembled like twigs in a gale. He was not used to hard labor, and his muscles had nothing left to give.

"Can't," he panted. "Can't . . . do this."

I glared at him. "Push."

"Am."

The weight of the jar grew. He wasn't pushing. His paws were flat against the side of the jar, and his eyes were closed. His mouth hung open. His breath came in heaving gasps. He was giving up. I saw it like a dark shadow on his face.

Anger rose along my spine, and I reached out with one paw and grabbed the fur behind his neck. His eyes opened.

"You want to die?" I asked.

He didn't answer. How dare he? After only a day on the docks? The Tira-Norans suffered weeks and months of agony, were tortured brutally before succumbing to exhaustion. Worse, he knew where my mother was!

Not a chance! I thought. *Not before you tell me.*

Through clenched teeth I said, "Where's Edina?"

When he didn't answer I gave his head a shake, though the jar was still closing the gap, shoving my knees higher and closer.

He shook his head. "Don't know."

"Think! She cooks for Hammah! Where in the palace does she do that?"

He looked down into the shrinking space beneath us.

"Please!" I said. "Tell me before it's too late."

He turned his head, his eyes sad and faraway, as though I had just said something cruel.

In the corner of my eye, beyond the wide open warehouse door and the slick, graying stumps of the quay, a black figure rose from the river and shook itself in a spray of water. She stepped into the warehouse with the slow, soundless grace of the lizard, trailing puddles from her webbed feet and iridescent tail.

I saw myself then, shaking the head of a dying mouse and demanding answers even as I was about to be crushed by the weight of a jar. I saw someone I did not know, someone even Father would not have recognized.

What kind of monster had I become?

Newbie was no Cadridian. Not any more. He was a slave—like me. A mouse who knew nothing about life and death. A mouse caught up in circumstances beyond his choosing, about to surrender his soul to eternity.

I drew my paw back and shook my head as disgust overwhelmed me.

"Push," I said. "Just push. Don't die."

His eyelids fluttered. "Not . . . palace," he said. "Hammah's mansion. Opposite street. House of . . . elm."

He drew a tiny breath and his eyes rolled back in his head. His face whitened. His feet slipped downward and he dropped into the gap, his face staring up at me without expression. The jar pressed against his lower legs and torso. One paw thrust upward. His mouth hung open.

The full weight of the jar squeezed against my legs. A numb feeling of nothingness crept up from my ankles, as though I were standing in frigid water.

Taskmasters screamed orders: "Push! Push! Push, you maggots!" Mice strained at the lip of the jar. Slaves who neither knew me nor cared for me struggled to save my life.

It occurred to me that they were trying to save my life. Is a slave more than a product? I wondered. More than canned peanut butter?

My legs jerked like a pair of hooked fish. The iron weight of the jar pressed against my feet, forcing my knees to my chest. The blue lid pressed so close I could grip it with my forepaws.

The world lost its color. Fog seeped over everything. The harsh curses of the taskmasters faded in my ears.

Kalla padded into the center of the warehouse. Her lower jaw hung down like a dog's, as though she were panting.

No, not panting. Smiling. At me.

It was a wicked smile, like that of an executioner who whistles as he whets his axe.

"Mine," Kalla whispered.

Outside, more shapes rose dripping from the water.

The disgust I had felt in seeing myself intensified as I stared into her black eyes.

Agony rose from my knees as my straining muscles gave out. Paws reached under my armpits, tugged uselessly against the grip of gravity.

From the water. To the water. My mind rose from my body and stared out at the open door. Kalla is the water and the water is Kalla. Nothingness. Escape.

"You're like me now," Kalla said. "You will be like me forever."

I shook my head, though my neck was a lump of wood on my shoulders. Despair settled over me like a wet wool blanket. Was it true? Was I already like her? A nothing filled with nothing? Was I as cold and empty as the black waters of the river?

The paws tugging at my body let go.

The jar forced my knees into my chest, squeezed the air from my lungs in a slow, heavy rush.

"Push!"

Father's voice whispered in my ear, so faint I almost couldn't hear it, so close it seemed to be coming from inside of me. *"Kalla . . .,"* Father said, *". . . is a twit."*

A spark, half a hiccup of light and hope, fluttered in my stomach. A single seed of something simple and pure and honest took root and began to grow.

"Tell her that for me," Father said.

Joy bloomed.

"No," I said to the dripping cartilage of her lips, though my mouth no longer worked properly, and my tongue did not seem to move. "Not yours. Never. I will never again let myself be like you. I am going to—"

Hammah's mansion. Opposite street. House of the elm.

I stepped from the sagging wisp of fur that was my body and stood back as slaves were summoned from the palace to help force the jar over and free the two bodies trapped behind it. Below the shelf, someone screamed obscenities at the taskmasters for killing two slaves in one day. *Someone cares!* I thought, which struck me as funny in a distant, detached sort of way, because it wasn't true. No one cared about slaves. They cared about having to replace slaves.

The physical sensation was almost identical to what I felt the day I ran from Tira-Nor to the outskirts of Cadrid. (How odd that sounds to natural ears!) But this time I felt no emotion whatsoever, and it took no act of will to live suspended above my flesh.

I lived. My body lived. We just lived separately. I accepted these facts, but I could not explain them. No wonder AlBaer spoke in riddles! The words one needs to describe all of reality have not been invented.

Slaves carried me down the shelf and out onto the quay, where the river lapped blackly at its rotting wood. By this time the sun had set and moonlight struck the surface of the river in shafts of blue steel. They dumped me unceremoniously onto the deck and waited until a taskmaster came over and looked into my unfocused eyes.

"Twopence," he said. He motioned to another taskmaster. "Surrah Hammah must be told. He will not be happy."

No? And why will Hammah not be happy? Does my life matter to him somehow?

The taskmaster motioned to the two closest slaves, who sighed and hoisted me by the wrists and ankles to the edge.

Shapes swam in the water.

I shuddered.

I was walking between worlds now, and the thought of going to one or the other was almost as terrifying as the thought of going to neither.

Kalla's obscene head appeared above me, hanging down from a dark cloud that spread across the face of the moon. "Mine," she said in a cold whisper.

I tried to point a finger at her, but my arms would not move. "I know where my mother is," I said.

"Your mother?" Her lips opened in a sneer. "Your mother is with me."

They heaved my body into the chilling blackness.

Chapter Twenty-One

Atwania

The water tugged at my skin, but my body refused to sink. Webbed fingers clutched at my back and sides, gliding over my tail with clammy precision. I neither shuddered nor shrank from their touch, though every instinct within me revolted.

Something vast and inexplicable—the same force that buoyed my body just at the crest of the waves and kept water from spilling down my throat—also held me fast, immobilized, and staring heavenward.

Stars wandered the cold tracks of the night sky as the current pulled me past the quays, past the taller buildings of man-houses. Trees rose up on the banks of the river. The sound of the falls receded to a distant roar.

When at last my back scraped the bank of the river, a slow feeling of warmth crept into my limbs, and suddenly the buoyant sensation disappeared. I sat up with a splash and backed out of the water, trailing moss.

A moment passed before I found my bearings. I knew where Cadrid lay, though I didn't know how long it would take to get there. I had to get back.

Though the moon hung full and somber on the western horizon, I kept to open spaces. Foolish? Yes. But that night I felt nothing could harm me, even if owls did patrol those woods.

Occasionally, a dark shape would rise from the surface of the river and reach out with an open palm or a hooked claw, but I paid no attention. I had felt Kalla's cold caress—now that it had passed the sensation did make me shudder—but she had not claimed me. I still walked the earth. Her jaws and fingers were, on that night at least, powerless to pull me into her domain.

Before dawn I crept back to the outskirts of Cadrid from the downriver side. No sentries guarded the streets. Presumably, the city's best fighters were still marching to Tira-Nor to wreak vengeance over PaTri's well-deserved fate.

A cool wind swept off the river, but the warmth in my limbs still lingered and I felt no chill. I padded through dark shadows and darted down brick-paved streets cracked by weeds until I saw the dark roof of the palace rising over the city.

A few more blocks and the building I sought revealed itself under purple starlight. A single elm jutted from the earth, its trunk so close to the foundation that it seemed to split the cement blocks. Hammah's mansion.

Two mice guarded the entry, a broken pane of stained glass in the window by the massive double front doors. They looked bored and tired, but were both awake.

I slipped through the hole and strode past them, but if they noticed me, they gave no sign. I might have been dreaming, but I felt no sensation of unreality. The wood steps under my paws were cool in the night air. I leapt from step to step, not caring about the scratch of my claws on the glossy surface.

The upstairs hallway ran the length of the house. Its arched ceiling spread above gold-framed oil paintings of men in stiff jackets and women in bright dresses.

Another guard stood watch at the end of the hallway, and he did not look bored. Powerfully built, he stood as immobile as the people in the paintings, his eyes narrow, his back to the closed door. I might have slipped under the door and confronted Hammah again, but voices stopped me.

"And he is dead?" Hammah said. His throaty cough came muffled but unmistakable from the other end of the hall.

"Certainly, Surrah. I checked him myself, Surrah. His eyes were fixed."

"And what did you do with him?"

"Surrah, we gave him to Kalla. May Kalla be as slow as he is quick. I watched his body descend."

I padded closer to the room from which the sounds emanated.

"Make amends to his master," Hammah said. "Something appropriate."

"Yes, Surrah Hammah."

"And find me a new—"

I ducked under the door and approached Hammah. His ever-present guards turned when they saw me and scowled.

It took a moment for that to register. They had seen me. Whatever power animated my flesh, lifted me over current and stone, and shielded me from the eyes of guards was fading.

Or was it?

A body lay on the floor in one corner. Hammah stood over it, the taskmaster from the warehouse at his side, eyes popping.

At me.

"Surrah Hammah," I said.

Hammah turned, put one paw to his chest, and coughed a long, hacking cough as his eyes bulged. "Twopence," he said. "They tell me—for the second time—that you are dead."

"It's true," I answered. "Twopence died in your warehouse, at the paws of cruel taskmasters and a cruel god. But I, Eli, son of LiDel, am not dead, and I have come to ask you again to honor—"

"No," he interrupted, clapping his paws for silence. "You will not talk of honor in this room. And neither shall I. Not now. FairKhi." He indicated the taskmaster, who bowed deeply. "You looked in his eyes, but here he stands! Leave us. Do not appear before me again or I will feed you to Kalla myself!"

FairKhi dipped his head in a hurried bow and scampered under the doorway.

Hammah's guards spread out in a semicircle behind me.

"Will you speak to me of Tira-Nor?"

"I will not, Surrah Hammah."

Iron paws gripped my neck, but Hammah waved the brute off.

"Very well, Eli, son of LiDel. The price is paid now, regardless. I have nothing to offer you, and you refuse to meet my demands." His face was blank, inscrutable.

"I have toiled in your death camps, Surrah Hammah! And you do have something to offer!" One of the guards snarled at my insolence, but I pressed on. "You know the whereabouts of my . . . of the slave called Edina."

"I did," he answered, "until last night. She was making my supper when Kalla came for her."

Disbelief hung heavy in my mind. "What do you mean?" I asked, though I really knew.

"I called her Atwania. Most favored of my servants." He pointed to the body in the corner. "In another life, some called her Edina. You, perhaps, when you were still a kit."

I walked past him to the body and stared.

Even after all these years—and even though I couldn't remember what she looked like—still I recognized her. She lay on her side, legs thrust out as though stretching for a walk. Memories flooded back to me in waves. Night songs, a cooing voice, smiling eyes, the way she tilted her head and rocked when she was happy.

But older now. The fur on her back was cold to the touch. Her shoulders were mounded with age. Her whiskers, thin as razor wire, were white as starlight.

Rage flooded my being. I turned to face Hammah, my jaws clenched, but he was already plodding to the doorway. In my path stood six of his bodyguards, scowling like jackals.

One of them looked for a moment at my mother's dead body, and I thought I saw a flicker of disdain twist his snout.

It was all the excuse I needed. Whatever power remained from the world between fell away in an instant as I launched myself at his face.

It took three of them to pull me off him.

Chapter Twenty-Two

Glyn the Small

"Why," Dawna asked for the third time that morning, "are you so strong?"

Glyn lay in a corner of RuHoff's cave with his back to the cold surface of the wall and let the chill of the rock seep into his limbs. *Stone,* he thought. *I am a stone. I am Glyn the Stone and mere words do not touch me.*

Just above his head a narrow shelf of rock jutted from the wall in a shallow frown. Even the walls were unhappy.

He spoke without looking up. "ElShua made me that way."

This was the answer he had given twice already, though the morning had only just begun. The sun still threw warm morning light into the mouth of the cave.

Glyn always gave the same answer. It had become a kind of family ritual. When she asked him again in a few moments, he would say, "ElShua made me that way," and she would thrust out her lower jaw and narrow her eyes and turn away for a while. Then, when peace had almost stolen back into the cave, and his mind had almost relaxed enough to think of something else, she would ask the question again. Like water pounding against rock. And he would repeat the same answer, his voice as hard and cold as the stone at his back. And in the silence that followed he would wonder again which element was really the stronger in the end, and which of them was indeed made of stone.

"You aren't telling me something," she said.

"Like what?"

"I don't know. But there's something."

Glyn tried to sink deeper into the wall. Of course he wasn't telling her something. She didn't love him, didn't even seem to like him. Why would he give her the secret of his strength?

He backed further against the wall, felt the crack that split the wall from floor to ceiling. Its edges made two jagged lines along the ridge of his back.

"Give me a hint," Dawna said.

Glyn sighed, wishing he could make himself small. If he were small, he would disappear into the crack and stay there until he remembered what it was like not to be always irritated.

"You won't even give me a hint?" Dawna asked.

"Why do you keep pestering me about this?"

"Why do you write poems for everyone but me?"

"Is that what's bothering you?"

"What's bothering me," she said, "is that you keep secrets. You save the best of yourself for everyone else. You don't really love me!"

"Love you?" Glyn looked up from the corner. "I creep when you want me to run!" he said. "I fly when I should crawl! I leap when there's much to be done. You die when you've had my all."

Dawna cocked her head to one side and stared at him for a long time. "What are you talking about?" she asked finally.

"You wanted a poem," Glyn answered.

Dawna frowned and poked him in the chest. "That's not a poem," she said. Her eyes jabbed at him like fish-hooks. "It's a riddle!"

Glyn laughed. "It is a poem and a riddle."

"What good is a riddle I can't understand?"

"It is the glory of noblemice to unravel riddles," Glyn said.

"Unravel it for me!"

He turned his face to the wall, feeling as though he were about to explode. He felt the edges of the crack against his forehead.

"You don't love me!" Dawna said at his back. "You are a beast!"

ElShua, Glyn prayed silently, *this wife is driving me mad. If you love me, open up this rock and let me hide in it. If you love me, make me small!*

Silence.

Starting low but growing louder, a sound like tearing cloth hissed from the crack as it widened around his head. He pushed his shoulders through and shoved against the floor of the cave with both paws. The rock groaned, stretched, creaked like an old tree in the wind.

Dawna shrieked.

Glyn looked back long enough to say, "Time. Time is the answer to the riddle."

The crack snapped shut, leaving a jagged slash of light. Dawna's shriek died away to silence.

Glyn stood in a tall, narrow tunnel with no visible ceiling. The walls followed the slash of the crack, cutting up into the darkness of the stone. He stepped deeper into the rock, following the high walls of the tunnel, his fingers brushing against them on either side.

In the distance, thin stalks of light streamed down from somewhere high above. Glyn walked forward until he came to a dead end. He closed his eyes and relished the cool silence. Peace settled over him like a blanket. Gradually, all of the rage that had built up in him drained away. He felt it leave, swirling away down his neck, shoulders, back, knees, and paws. He felt warm and cold at the same time. He did not know whether ElShua had made him smaller or the crack bigger; nor, in truth, did he care. He felt as though he did not know who or where he was. Then again, he felt that he knew exactly who and where he was, but for the first time.

I'm not a stone, he thought. I'm a hypocrite. Did I really just say to ElShua, "If you love me?" Did I really just pray the very words that are driving me mad?

He looked at the light streaming down. "ElShua," he said. "I am sorry I said if."

He stood there in the crack for many hours as the sun inched its way across the narrow floor and up the wall.

When light yellowed the stone at eye level, Glyn pressed one paw against it. With his claw he scratched a series of RuHoff-like pictures into the solid rock.

I do not want to be strong any more.

He stared at the picture-words and knew that he must go back out of the crack. Dawna would worry about him. Or, if not about him, about herself. Maybe she didn't love him, but she did need him.

He heard a sound like a cough and turned in the narrow space to see the Ghost Badger standing there above him, half in and half out of the wall. Light fell from the tips of his fur, gleaming against the blackness of his body. His eyes were pools of fire.

The badger held up one finger, then scratched a message in the rock on the opposite wall, in letters taller than Glyn's body.

You never were strong.

Twilight flickered at the cave entrance when the crack opened and Glyn stepped back out into the shadows of the cave.

Dawna made a sound like a hiccup when she saw him. She didn't ask him where he had been, or if he was all right. She didn't even ask him why he was weeping.

Chapter Twenty-Three

Surrah Hammah

"Eli, son of LiDel," a voice called under the door.

I blinked and sat up, my back stiff. The beating I had received at the hands of Hammah's guards had done no permanent damage, but every inch of my body felt bruised.

A mouse poked his nose under the door but did not enter. "Prepare yourself," he said. "You are to stand before His Eminence, the Lord of Cadrid, this very morning."

"The king?" I asked. "What's he want with me?"

The nose disappeared without answering.

I sighed and slowly lay back. Sunlight streamed from a window high in the wall, but the room was otherwise empty. I'd been kept here for two days, though they had taken Mother's body during the first night.

Had she been dumped in the river? Did Kalla come for her? Or did she walk between? Had she found some way into ElShua's Garden at last?

Hours later two guards came and escorted me out of the room, down the broad oak steps, and out the front door into the street.

We entered the palace on the north side, climbing a long ramp that led to an open doorway. My battered muscles ached and every step left me panting for breath.

We stopped at an archway as my escort explained to a dozen guards who I was and that I had been summoned. Then we entered the massive Great Hall of the palace, and I forgot my private pain. Marble pillars caught the light that shone from high windows set in alcoves above the green marble of the floor. Statues of men, chiseled from gleaming columns of pure white, stood between the pillars. Their features were eerily lifelike, and though they loomed above us, their eyes did not look down, but gazed off into the distance. It was as though we had come into the presence of ancient gods, frozen for eternity in a moment of time.

At the far end of the Great Hall a single statue, shorter than the others but just as bulky, formed the centerpiece of the hall. A man knelt on a patch of marble grass. He held his hat in one hand over his chest, and in the other he held out what seemed to be a single seed. Before him, chiseled from the same white marble, a mouse rose up to accept the seed with outstretched paws.

Mice gathered before the statue on a tasseled rug woven of blood-red fibers as they all peered into what looked like a tent with no roof. Screens of colored silk hung from wooden frames in a semicircle at the center of the rug. The mice on the rug gathered at the open end and stared in silence at something I could not see.

They stepped aside when they saw us. My escort paused and bowed to the statue of the mouse and man. One of them grabbed my neck. "Bow!" he hissed, jerking my head down.

He cleared his throat. "Surrah, may I present Eli, son of LiDel, as commanded."

He stepped aside, revealing the curious stares of the courtiers and nobility.

On a mat of bundled silks lay Hammah. His face was flushed, his fur matted with sweat. "Come," he said, motioning with one paw.

I stepped closer. "Surrah Hammah?"

"I am told that you walk between the worlds."

The fur on my spine prickled. How did he know?

"Yes, Surrah Hammah, I have done this."

He nodded. "And I am told that you can heal me."

I looked around at the Cadridian nobility, but their faces were all turned down. They seemed to be pretending not to hear what we said. As though it were a humiliation Hammah must suffer alone. "Who told you that?"

He scowled. "Never mind who told me! Can you or can't you?"

"I can't," I said. "And wouldn't if I could."

Someone gasped behind me.

Hammah's brows gathered in the center. He pursed his lips. "Wouldn't!"

"You ask me for life and health? Why should I give you anything?"

He raised himself to a sitting position, then broke into a fit of coughing. His eyes were fixed in an angry stare, though it seemed he was not so much angry at me but at the sudden powerlessness into which he had fallen.

Since he did not answer, I pressed on. "You, Surrah Hammah, kept my mother as a slave! Took her from me! Stole my childhood. And if not you, then your servants, which amounts to the same thing. You refused even to let me see her, when a day or two might have meant everything."

My voice rose with my temper. I expected the guards to finish the beating they had begun two days earlier, but they did not interfere. "You had mercy at your fingertips," I continued, "and yet you wouldn't move a whisker to help. Even now it is the same. Even in your need, you will not help those within your power."

His back straightened. "Whom have I ignored?"

"Are there not dozens of mice working themselves to death in your warehouse this very moment? How many will die this week? How many will be taken by Kalla because you must have cream for your table?"

"But—" his mouth worked furiously. "Those are not mice! Those are slaves."

"I was your slave, Surrah Hammah! How can you ask for help from such as me?"

His eyes narrowed. All at once he clapped his paws and said, "DaiKim!"

A mouse came forward and kneeled, head down. "Surrah Hammah?"

"Stop the work in the warehouse at once."

"And at the cedar mill," I said.

Hammah's eyes registered surprise. His mouth twitched. "And at the cedar mill," he repeated.

"At once, Surrah Hammah!" DaiKim said, and scurried off.

"Now," Hammah said, turning his face to mine.

"Now?"

"You will heal me."

"Two days ago, perhaps," I said. "But not now. Now it is too late."

"Why too late?" he asked, his voice loud in the silence.

Proud Hammah! Proud Cadrid! City of darkness and wealth and honor. With a heart of cold, white marble. "Because you took my mother," I answered. I knew the guards would kill me for it, but I didn't care.

I turned my back on him and looked for some way to escape. A few mice threw furtive glances my direction.

"Twopence," Hammah whispered. Something in his voice stopped me from leaping into the gap and bolting for the doors. Something familiar and marvelous. Something impossible. His voice sounded exactly like Father's.

Slowly, I turned back to him.

"Not for all the wealth of Cadrid would I do this. But for these, my children—" He spread out both paws, indicating the nobles gathered around us.

He scooted his black bulk to the edge of the cushions and lowered himself to one knee. "Twopence.

Eli, son of LiDel. Apprentice to AlBaer, Seer of Tira-Nor. I, Surrah Hammah, Steward of the Realm—" He stopped, nodding slowly, as though to draw out of himself words that he could hardly bear to say, "—do humbly beg for your assistance."

Behind me, mice began to weep. His children?

"You have mercy at your fingertips, Eli," he said. "Will you now move a whisker to help?"

All the strength of my anger dissolved as I stared down into his proud, pleading eyes. In that moment he was more than a ruler, more than a steward or a slave-trader or a tyrant. He was a father humiliated before his children. A dying mouse with no hope for the future.

I looked from face to face and saw, to my great shame, a palace of lost souls. *This is Cadrid,* I thought. *Every mouse here is a slave. Even Hammah.*

Power rose within me—a living, tangible thing as real as the sunlight streaming through the arched windows.

"Surrah Hammah," I said quietly, "I cannot heal you. Only ElShua can do that. But perhaps there is a way. Are you willing to do anything?"

Slowly, he raised himself back to the couch and gave a short series of coughs behind one fist. "I have just now done more than any lord protector in Cadridian history."

"But," I said, "It is not enough. Your people live waiting for the jaws of Kalla to close. You say you want life, but you worship death."

"Kalla is inexorable."

"Then why do you try to cheat her now?"

He stared at me for a moment, then said. "What more must I do?"

"Come with me," I said.

I did not wait for his response, but pushed my way through the crowd and padded toward the double doors and the ramp that led down to the quays. All the long way I expected to be tackled by angry guards, and in truth I doubted he would follow. But I heard gasps, and Hammah's cough, and when I reached the entry I could no longer restrain myself. I turned and saw that his guards had put him on a litter and were carrying him across the green tiles. His face might have looked pitiful if it weren't so commanding and, in some inexpressible way, humbled.

They followed me all the way around the back of the warehouse and out onto the wooden platform. Wood creaked in the current. On the far pier a white bird swatted the air with tousled wings before leaping into flight.

Hammah rose from the litter and stepped slowly and heavily toward the edge, refusing the outstretched arms of the mice around him.

"The river," I said, nodding toward the lapping waves. "That's what you fear. Death. The great void."

He drew a long breath, his nostrils flaring. "I fear nothing."

"No?"

"No," he said through clenched teeth.

"Not even weakness?" I pointed at the nobles, his children. "Losing your strength in front of them?"

His eyes narrowed for just a moment. I thought he might turn to go, but he merely shrugged. "I do not fear weakness. I despise it."

I stepped to the edge of the quay. "And what about Kalla? Do you fear her?"

"Kalla and the river are one."

"Yes," I said. "And twice she has swallowed me, only to spit me back out. I am alive because there is something greater than Kalla. His name is ElShua. And if you want to escape the black void, you must fling yourself into Him. You must trust while the choice is still yours."

Understanding broke over him suddenly. His eyes widened. "Go living into the water?" His voice rose unexpectedly high, the sound of an incredulous kit.

"Yes, Surrah Hammah."

"And—" He looked over the edge of the quay. "You promise I will come back out alive?"

I shrugged. "Would my promise change anything?"

He stared out at the black waves, unblinking, mesmerized.

I said, "I will go with you."

But still he did not speak.

"And there is this," I added. "It is not really a matter of *if,* but of *when*. Either you go into those waves with hope, or someone will fling you against your will when all that is left to you is despair."

I held out one paw. He looked down at it, and then back out at the waves, his face frozen in a mask of indecision. I reached out further and clamped his paw into my own. The contact seemed to snap him into reality. I wondered how many mice had dared to touch him before. The thought made me inexplicably sad.

How strange, I thought, just before we jumped. *I don't even like him!*

Chapter Twenty-Four

Kalla

I rose to the surface first.

Hammah came up sputtering, his black fur clinging to the wrinkled skin of his neck, his paws beating madly at the water even as his shoulders heaved with great, hacking coughs.

His paw had slipped from mine when we struck the water, so I grabbed madly for it, but his motions were too erratic. I tried again, and this time his flailing arms sent a gout of water into my face and down my throat.

Here below the falls the river moved more slowly, and yet the quay was slipping past, just beyond reach. Mice gathered at the edge and looked down at us. Some shouted commands. Most just stared, wide-eyed.

I took a deep breath and dove under, coming up behind him. We would never be able to climb the piers, but I had to do something to stop Hammah's panic. I shoved him in the back, my hind legs kicking at the current.

He let out a throaty scream and then hit the last pier with his enormous belly and face.

A layer of river moss thickened the wood with black slime, but Hammah sank his claws into it and was able to keep himself from sinking. I paddled up next to him and grabbed hold of the post. Mouse shadows fell through the chinks in the platform and scurried over the surface of the water.

Hammah let out a final weak cough and then took a deep breath, his eyes closed. He did not look at me when he spoke. "You brought me here to kill me."

I shook the water from my eyes and stared at the dark, misshapen forms that were gliding in a slow circle around us. "Yes."

"Why?"

"It's what you wanted."

His eyes opened and he stared hard at me before nodding.

"You killed Twopence," I said. "And I must kill Surrah Hammah. If you want to live, it is the only way."

"And if I do not want to live?"

"Then no one can help you. Not even ElShua."

He looked downriver, his face suddenly haggard. "It would be easy not to fight any more." He looked up at the shadows of his children on the quay. "To let go of everything."

His upturned face caught the light of the afternoon sun, and in an instant I understood the mystery of Hammah, what I had been puzzling over for days. "The king!" I said.

He looked at me, surprised. "What's that?"

"It's you. You're the king of Cadrid."

"I am no such thing," he said. "RajHa is king of Cadrid. RajHa the Inexorable, the Mighty, the Undying. He has been king since before I was born."

RajHa. White-faced, frozen, forever reaching up to take a seed from the hand of a man. "RajHa," I said, "is a marble statue."

"And the only mouse," Hammah said, "who has ever received offerings from men."

I smiled, suddenly giddy. "You've tried to be like him, but it hasn't worked. You are not made of stone."

"No," he said wearily. He looked away, his face a mask of pain and sadness.

"Thus—" I reached for his paw. "—You live."

A current passed through my paw into his. He let go of the pier and stared down beneath the surface of the water as the river tugged at us and pulled us away from the quay. He no longer fought the water; neither did he sink.

We floated lazily, our shoulders and heads fully above the waves, as though we stood on firm ground.

"Take my other paw," I said, "and don't let go."

Hammah's face froze, but though we faced each other, he did not look at me. He stared down, below the surface of the water. Fear traced its mark across his brow, stiffening his body. His paws clenched mine in an iron grip.

He saw what I saw. Kalla's fish-mouth swirling around us. Her eyes like black glass staring from nothing into nothing as smaller green shapes danced and wove in a terrible and chaotic rhythm of fear, without pattern or purpose, around her toad-like face. Webbed hands reached from the darkness and touched our backs, our legs, our bellies. The touch sucked life and meaning and hope out of our souls and replaced these things—or rather, tried to replace these things—with the madness.

We both felt it. Hatred oozed around us in a vast current. It swept over our skin with icy, unclean fingers that seemed desperate, and yet unable, to squeeze.

Kalla found no grip.

Behind us, the mice on the quay shouted.

Slowly, wonder crept over Hammah's face. He lifted his eyes and looked searchingly into mine. "Is it . . .?"

I smiled at him and began to giggle. "Kalla," I said, "is nothing."

He made a choking noise, and for a moment I thought he was about to go into another spasm of coughing. Instead, his lower jaw dropped and a series of hiccups erupted from his throat. Then a grin spread itself across his snout and his chest shook.

"You're . . . laughing?" I asked.

He closed his eyes and bellowed mirth at the sky as we drifted to the shore, our paws still locked. "Nothing nothing nothing," he said. "Kalla is nothing. Nothing to be afraid of, nothing to dread, nothing but bluster and wind and empty lost words—" His voice caught in his throat as we hit the bottom of the river and all buoyancy left us.

We had not drifted very far. We were still within the city of Cadrid. Empty buildings towered near the shoreline, and before us a gravel road rose up from the water and led to a weed-forested parking lot. We were standing in what must once have been a launch for small boats.

"Had she not been a servant, a commoner of Tira-Nor, I would have married her," Hammah said. He looked at the blue sky and green smear of trees on the horizon as though for the first time. "I was very fond of her."

"My mother?"

He didn't answer directly, but said, "Do you know what Atwania means?"

I shook my head.

"Most favored. My court assumed I meant that she was the most favored of my servants, but that was not true."

I started to help him ashore, but he pulled his paws out of mine and splashed toward the bank alone. Once on land he shook himself and patted down the sparse black fur on the top of his head.

He looked down at his paws and then back up at me as I joined him. He held his paws to his chest, and then touched his head for a moment, and then his chin. "Can I believe it?" he asked.

"You are not coughing."

He smiled again, his expression so changed I might have been looking at a different mouse. "No. Nor is there a cough lurking in here," he thumped his chest, "waiting to erupt at every breath."

A crowd of mice approached, running, Hammah's bodyguard in the lead.

"Surrah Hammah!"

"Master!"

"You live!"

Hammah held up both paws, palms out, as they surrounded us. "Silence!" he roared.

Dozens of heads went down. The sound of water dripping from my fur and splatting against gravel was loud in the stillness.

"Be it decreed," Hammah said, "that Eli, son of LiDel, apprentice to AlBaer of Tira-Nor, has ransomed his life according to the ancient code of RajHa by healing Surrah Hammah, Steward of the Realm. In payment of our life-debt, we pronounce him a free mouse. From this day forward he may travel within or without our lands, and must be accorded every courtesy. Let it be announced swiftly in every corner of Cadrid."

"Yes, Surrah Hammah!" the gathered mice answered.

"Excellent!" a familiar voice said from the top of the gravel drive. I turned to see a wiry stick of a mouse standing there, his fur blowing gently in the wind. "But what of the mice of Tira-Nor?"

It was AlBaer.

Chapter Twenty-Five

Alone

"Told you I'd come again later," AlBaer said as we paraded back to the palace in a long line. Hammah refused to be carried in his litter, but instead rumbled at the head of the column of twittering nobility.

AlBaer and I followed at the rear of the party, though his old legs seemed to have no difficulty keeping pace with the younger Cadridians.

"I thought you forgot about me."

His eyes drooped. "Why would you think something like that?"

"They made me a slave."

"No, Eli, they captured you. There is a difference. You needed to feel the lash, though I am sorry it cut so deep. All your life you've only had one master—yourself. And what a miserable taskmaster he is! I know; mine is just as bad."

Ahead of us, Hammah skirted the ramp and mounted the palace steps, holding his paws aloft in triumph at the top.

"I found my mother," I said.

"Did you?" AlBaer seemed genuinely pleased for a moment. Then, without me having to explain anything, his old whiskers wilted and his brows knotted together. "Ah. Well. I am sorry for that."

I stopped in the road and spoke to his back. "Why didn't you come sooner?"

He stopped and turned toward me. "There was something you needed to do without me." He nodded ahead to Hammah. "That would not have happened otherwise."

"So what?" I exploded. "I might have had a chance to see her. To speak with her. Tell her—"

AlBaer took a hesitant step toward me, his expression full of pity.

That irritated me. "Doesn't that matter too?"

"You've seen Cadrid, Eli. You've felt the darkness they live in. Do you not understand it better now, for all your suffering?"

I looked around at brown brick buildings and cracked streets. "No," I said. "In fact, I'm more confused than when I first arrived. I thought you were going to make me an apprentice, AlBaer, but the only thing you've taught me is that I don't know anything!"

He smiled gently. "Then you have learned the most important thing."

◆ ◆ ◆

Hammah paced the red carpet like a tiny panther, his eyes hungry, his mouth set in a firm line. "What did you come for, eh? Master AlBaer? Seer of Tira-Nor? What would you have me do? This apprentice of yours is a scoundrel!" Here he glared at me in mock irritation. "Never had so much trouble with a slave. Had to free him to be rid of him. And then you show up. Just when the day was going splendidly." He stopped pacing and pointed one finger at AlBaer. "So. How do you plan to spoil it? What do you want?"

AlBaer's face remained placid. "I came for him." He pointed at me. "I came to get my apprentice back."

Hammah seemed genuinely surprised. "Of course. And to show our gratitude for your service in sending him to us, we shall welcome you to Cadrid." He turned to the courtiers. "Let it be decreed that both AlBaer, Seer of Tira-Nor, and Eli, son of LiDel, are guests of the realm. They shall take up residence in my mansion and eat at my table. They are free to go where they wish, and shall be shown all courtesy. Let it be done!"

A few mice scampered off; the others bowed.

AlBaer wore a look of puzzlement.

"You understand," Hammah said, "that you cannot go back to Tira-Nor."

"Why?" I asked, half-expecting a rebuke from AlBaer. None came.

"Tira-Nor is destroyed. Or about to be. My army moves against it even now. I gave strict orders to my generals. Were you to return, you would be killed."

I imagined the mice of Cadrid storming the gate holes of Tira-Nor and encountering wall-stones for the first time. Hammah's arrogance, as innocent and natural as it might be, irritated me. "You assume your army will win."

"Of course." Hammah said. "We have never lost a battle."

"If you're so sure, why did you ask me about Tira-Nor's defenses?"

He frowned. "I learned much about Tira-Nor's defenses when I was there. But I wanted to learn something about you."

I stared in silence as the meaning of his words swept over me. Rage boiled in my veins.

AlBaer must have sensed as much. He reached out and grabbed my shoulder with one wiry paw. "You will, of course, call off the attack on Tira-Nor."

"It is too late," Hammah said. "My messengers could never reach General KoTsu in time."

"But you agree the attack must be stopped?"

Hammah hesitated, then nodded slowly. "It is my will."

"Thank you, Surrah Hammah," AlBaer said. "Eli will deliver your message. It is our duty to return to Tira-Nor, regardless of the fate that awaits us there."

Hammah drew himself to his full height. "And if we forbid it? If King RajHa would have you stay?"

AlBaer's fingers dug into my flesh. He turned me toward the crowd of kneeling courtiers and cast his response over one shoulder. "Neither King RajHa nor Lord Hammah is my master. Come, Eli!"

He pushed me forward into the gawking crowd, which parted before us.

A sound like a gust of wind filled my ears, drowning Hammah's response. The court of Cadrid swam in liquid circles before us, face blending against face as the noise of a whirlwind grew.

Darkness descended, and from the darkness a path of warm, yellow light.

My steps were slow and heavy, as though I carried a great weight, but always AlBaer's hand gripped my shoulder, pushing me forward and down, deeper into the unknown.

At last the floor fell away and I collapsed onto my knees in a dark but oddly familiar place. A slanting blade of light haloed the earthen floor.

"I don't have much time," AlBaer said. "The Cadridian army is almost upon us. A day or two at most. King Ahaz must be warned."

"Where are we?" I asked in a shaky voice. I might have known the answer had the experience seemed less dreamlike. In those days—in spite of all that I had seen and done—I still imagined there is a great difference between what is possible and what is not. Power flowed in my limbs, vibrating like a spiderweb in a stiff breeze, and then subsided.

"RuHoff's cave," AlBaer said. "Where else?"

"I don't know, Cadrid maybe?"

He grinned. "I suggest you stay here. The king will

not have forgiven you for what happened at the Spring Festival."

"But I didn't do anything!"

"True," he agreed, padding to the entrance. "Life is like that. Those who do nothing always get the worst of it."

"Wait a minute!" I said angrily.

He turned, surprised. "Yes?"

"What just happened?"

"Whatever do you mean?"

"We were in Cadrid. In the court of Hammah, arguing about Tira-Nor, and now we're back in RuHoff's cave."

"You're surprised? But you've done this before."

I exploded. "Yes, with your help!"

"I don't understand you, Eli."

"Don't . . . don't understand?" I had trouble talking. The words stuck in my throat, blocked by a great lump of rage that shook my fists and made a red mist of AlBaer's silhouette at the entrance of the cave. "It was that easy for you? And you waited five weeks to come get me?"

He didn't answer immediately, but cupped his chin in one paw and stared calmly at the floor of the cave. When he spoke, his voice sounded old and weary, and yet full of patience. "I came the moment you were ready for me, Eli. Had you waited any longer, I suppose I could not have come at all."

I stared at him, frustrated and speechless.

"You are a good lad," he said. "In some ways very much like your father."

He turned and disappeared into the sunlight.

I kicked a pebble into the corner of the cave and strode over to where he slept. His straw pallet lay matted into a compressed outline that matched his skinny frame. I kicked it into a heap and then ran over to the entrance, but he was already out of sight.

RuHoff's cave? All through my torment in Cadrid, had this sanctuary been so close? Close enough to touch?

I closed my eyes and sat on the cool dirt floor. Everything seemed so dreamlike and unreal. Had I really survived the Spring Festival? Had I really run all the way to Cadrid in a matter of moments, and returned even more quickly? Had I really escaped the Cadridian slave trade and swum the black waters of the Kalla River unharmed? Had it really been me doing those things, and not some other mouse?

And here I sat in RuHoff's cave, weak and frustrated as ever, squatting in the dirt like a beetle, perhaps in the very spot where Glyn the Strong had written his best riddles.

I opened my eyes and stared at the ceiling, blinking away the shadows. But it was not Glyn's words I saw poised above me.

Wroth sells disguises.

"Indeed he does," Father whispered in a voice not unlike AlBaer's. *"And mice buy them. Which is why there must be seers."*

Disguises?

Not AlBaer. Me. I was the one wearing a disguise. Trying to be something—someone—I wasn't.

I am either a seer's apprentice or I'm not, I thought. *Probably not. But AlBaer thinks I am. So why should I run from it? Why should I put a mask on the face of Eli the Apprentice? Why do I fight it?*

"He's not coming back," I said out loud. The words popped into my head like sparks from a hedge fire, and I knew it was true. "King Ahaz is going to kill him. He's not coming back."

I scrambled outside and up the sloping hill above the roof of the cave.

Dragonflies buzzed over fields of long summer grass that bristled in a hot breeze. A merciless afternoon sun hung in the cloudless sky, but I didn't feel the heat, even after I broke into a desperate sprint to the southern horizon.

◆ ◆ ◆

I found AlBaer standing just north of the Royal Gate, his thorny arms outstretched. I paused for a moment and drew a gasping breath before jogging toward him.

"King Ahaz!" AlBaer called. "I have a message for you. For the love of your people, would you hear it?"

Mice of the kingsguard stood in a pocket outside the shadow of the gate hole. One of them trotted a few steps toward AlBaer before stopping. He cupped one paw to his snout. "The king is coming, old mouse, but you won't like what he has to say."

AlBaer lowered his arms and turned towards me, his face split by a wide, joyous smile.

"What did you mean," I panted, "when you said . . . if I waited longer . . . you couldn't have come . . . at all?"

He drew a deep breath, his chest filling even as his

eyes closed. "Already I have overstayed my welcome, Eli. But I did hope you would follow me. For that, whatever was mine is yours." His eyes flicked open. "And now, I think you will no longer need me. Good—"

Something dark and heavy flashed before me, and AlBaer disappeared.

The mice of the kingsguard swore. They scrambled back into the shadow of the gate hole, pointing up with trembling fingers. I blinked, confused, craning my neck upward.

Grayfeather's wide, straggling wings flapped slowly against the earth. In his talons he grasped a limp figure that hung like a strip of old leather beneath his rising form.

I watched, dumbstruck and motionless, expecting the ancient bird to wheel about and glide to his nest above Round Top, but he didn't. His wings beat the air slowly, methodically, as he rose. He flew in a straight line into the sun until he was little more than a black dot against a sheet of blue silk.

And in the middle of the blue silk glimmered the fields of the north meadows, drenched in blood. Bodies of mice lay everywhere in the tall grass: kingsguard warriors, militia-mice, the nobles of the Greater and Lesser Families. Then the north meadows washed past my vision, and the emptiness of the heavens once again ran clear and blue as a winter stream.

I didn't notice the king standing in the gate hole, nor the squad of soldiers he sent to arrest me. I barely felt their hold on my arms. I don't remember the march to the Royal Gate, nor what they said. Whatever it was, I didn't answer.

My eyes were fixed on the now empty sky.

Chapter Twenty-Six

Glyn the Beast

"If you loved me," Dawna said, "you'd tell me your secret."

Glyn plugged his ears with his fingers. But Dawna was still talking to him. Her mouth moved, and he didn't have to read her lips to know what she said. You don't love me. If you loved me you'd tell me your secret. You're a beast!

He rose and stalked to the entrance of the cave.

"Where are you going?"

"Somewhere quiet."

"Why did you marry me?"

He looked at her. "I thought you loved me."

Her lower lip moved. She turned away from him and wept silently.

Glyn stared, puzzled. What had he said? It was the truth. He had thought she loved him. Her smile, the way she spoke, her dark brown eyes . . . "What's wrong?" he asked.

"Just—," she said, her shoulders heaving, "—just leave."

"I don't understand."

She turned suddenly, her face red. "You thought I loved you? That's why you married me?"

"Well, yes." Glyn said. "I mean—"

"Not because you loved me! Because you thought I loved you!"

Glyn stared at her as understanding flooded his whole body. Shame dug roots into the soil of his heart as he tried to think of something—anything—to say. At last he managed to squeak out a very soft "Oh."

"But I knew that all along," Dawna said. "You never could tell me you loved me." She sniffed and turned her back to him. "Because you don't."

He took a step toward her, reached out with one paw, then drew back. "I . . ." he said. He knew he ought to go to her, put his arms around her, tell her he was sorry. He knew he ought to say, "I love you, Dawna." But he didn't. Everything within him recoiled at the thought of saying those words. He knew what love was. He had seen it growing up. His parents loved well. Their lives were love. He refused to be party to such a monstrous lie. To dress up tolerance as something else, to put a mask over rejection, to call it love instead of dislike—or even hate. He couldn't do this. He wouldn't do this.

Tell Dawna he loved her? Impossible. He didn't love her. He didn't even like her.

But he had made a promise, and he owed her.

"I want to tell you something," he said.

Her whole body shook. She leaned forward sobbing. Her voice splintered when she spoke. "I . . . don't . . . want . . ."

"I am a beast," Glyn said.

". . . to hear it!"

"A beast," he said, "who mustn't eat raisins."

Chapter Twenty-Seven

The Trial

King Ahaz and Queen IsaBel squatted like toads on the earthen dais at the far end of the palace hall. He looked older and thinner, less sure of himself. The queen, too, looked different. Anxiety hung on her like an old rag, bunching her shoulders and darkening her face. When she moved, fear weighted her steps.

This time, Father was not there to force my head down. I felt no obligation to honor the murderous pond scum with a bow, so I walked as close to the platform as I dared and stopped without speaking.

They had summoned me. Let them speak first.

Ahaz narrowed his eyes at my fixed stare. I suppose my dislike for him stood plainly on my face. He spoke without pretense. "Where is your master? Where is AlBaer?"

"I don't know."

"He was here, outside the Royal Gate. He had a message for me. Then he disappeared."

I shrugged. "True enough."

IsaBel stole poisonously to the edge of the platform and spoke in a tone as cold as frost. "You will address the king as Your Highness or Your Majesty."

I ignored her. "Last I saw of AlBaer . . ." I paused for a moment, wondering how far I should push them. ". . . Your Highness, he was hanging from the talons of Grayfeather and rising into the southern sky."

Ahaz scowled. "What message did he have for me?"

"I don't know. He didn't tell me."

"What did he tell you?"

This was none of the king's business, but I decided against telling him so. Instead, I nodded indifferently. "He said good-bye. I think he knew it was going to happen."

Ahaz paced to the far wall and stroked his chin with one paw. He spoke softly, almost to himself. "That makes no sense. If he knew it was going to happen, why say that he had a message? Why stand out there in the open and make himself a target?" The king turned and padded back to me, eyeing me closely. "What aren't you telling me?"

I looked from his face to that of Queen IsaBel, and then back. "I would tell you, Your Majesty, but you don't want to hear it."

IsaBel stomped her hind paw. "Insolence!" she shrieked.

King Ahaz reached out with one paw and grabbed me by the throat. "I see AlBaer didn't teach you any manners." He leaned closer and let out a stream of sour breath into my face. "I won't ask again."

I should have been terrified, but compared to the treatment I endured at the claws of the Cadridian taskmasters, this seemed mild. The king's paws were soft as down, his claws manicured to a dull, smooth sheen.

"The Cadridian army is about to attack Tira-Nor," I said calmly. "They will approach from the north in two days or less. And they will spare no one. All in Tira-Nor will be killed or exiled."

His eyes narrowed, but showed no surprise. Of course, kingsguard scouts would have warned him already. But would such a mouse listen to reason, or end his days in denial?

"Why should Cadrid come here?"

"Because you failed to protect their priests at the Spring Festival," I said. "Your Majesty."

He let go of my neck and stepped back, his face ashen.

IsaBel gave a high, unpleasant giggle and swept across the dais to put a birdlike paw on the king's shoulder. "And how can you possibly know this?"

"The lord protector of Cadrid, Surrah Hammah, told me so himself."

"He told you?" she asked.

"Yes."

"When?"

I thought for a moment about how absurd the answer would sound. It took many weeks to travel between Tira-Nor and Cadrid. But I couldn't bring myself to lie, and didn't really want to.

I took a deep breath. "This morning," I said. "When I was in Cadrid."

◆ ◆ ◆

They ordered me bound and carried to the Great Hall for immediate trial. Two mice of the kingsguard dumped me in one corner and warned me to keep silent. Paws tied, I could not move, so I watched as the Great Hall swelled with onlookers and the royal prosecutor spoke in hushed tones to the king's inner circle of advisors and counselors.

The trial was to take place within the hour, a showpiece of the king's fairness. I played the role of the villain, the monster of the Spring Festival, brought home now to pay for my crimes. I was a scoundrel not content with betraying death; I had now led a once-friendly nation into war with the mice of Tira-Nor through lies and bribery. Eli, son of the traitor LiDel, who had led the army of Cadrid to the very gates of the place I had for so long called home.

I wondered what the mice of Tira-Nor really thought of "justice" that replaced evidence with entertainment and deliberation with urgency. Had the city fallen so far that a sham trial might be mistaken for the real thing by mice of common sense?

I couldn't—and wouldn't—believe it, even when the jury of commoners that huddled near the king's seat at the north wall stabbed their fingers at me and indicated with rude gestures that they wanted me executed. What else might they think? They had heard only the official version of my alleged crimes. None knew the truth.

The trial drew more attention than the Spring Festival. Mice jammed into the Great Hall and spilled into the corridors in all directions. The guards untied my wrists as the prosecutor recited the sizable list of charges against me.

I had no real chance of a fair trial. My crimes were fictional. What defense could I mount? What evidence could I present that couldn't be swatted aside with even more forceful lies?

They convicted me of the foulest treasons and infamies. They convicted me of murdering PaTri and the priests of Cadrid—though at the time my paws had been tied to a burning stake and I was too weak even to lift my own weight. They convicted me of spiriting away Master AlBaer, in spite of the testimony of those kingsguard warriors who had seen Grayfeather strike. And they convicted me of conspiracy to incite a war between Tira-Nor and Cadrid.

I listened to the charges and the evidence and the false witnesses with a sense of peace I could not explain. Tira-Nor was doomed, regardless of what happened at my trial.

"The prisoner will now rise to hear the decision of the jury," a voice said.

One of the guards kicked me in the ribs. I scrambled up and said, "You have not allowed me to speak."

"Quiet, you!" a voice said from the jury. A chorus of agreement erupted from the huddled jury.

"Quiet?!" I bellowed, bringing instant silence. "I have been nothing but quiet for two hours! Can you not listen for a moment? Or have the ancient laws of Tira-Nor been completely erased by the likes of him?" I pointed at the prosecutor. "A mouse who would as soon sell any of you to a Cadridian taskmaster as scratch his own backside."

Something like shame settled over the crowd. It is easy to hate someone with no face, no voice, no identity. When that someone becomes a person right in front of you, hatred loses its strength.

The prosecutor stroked the side of his chin with one lean finger. When he spoke, his voice burned through the hesitation of the crowd like dripping acid. "It is customary," he said slowly, "for a condemned mouse to be allowed to say something. However foolish his words may be."

I ignored him. I ignored the king and queen and their stooges who huddled in the sheltering light of glowstones thrown from the passage to the Kingsguard section of the city. I ignored the kingsguard mice, who watched from the northwest passages and seemed to regard the event as pure entertainment. I looked straight at the jury.

"It does not matter that the charges against me are vile, monstrous, and untrue. It does not matter that I was an apprentice to AlBaer. You didn't respect him. Why should you respect his apprentice? It does not matter that he came to give King Ahaz one final message before Grayfeather took him away. It doesn't matter because the king would not have listened. He still will not listen, and that will be his undoing.

"But you! Mice of Tira-Nor! You must listen, because your lives are at stake too. What King Ahaz does tomorrow will determine whether you live or die, stay here as free mice or suffer the lash of Cadridian taskmasters in an unknown land."

A few of the jury mice shifted uneasily. None met my gaze.

"Cadrid is coming!" I said. "I know this. I have seen her armies marching forth in battalions, and I know that wall-stones will not save you. The engineers of Cadrid know where to dig, how to get around your booby traps and fool's errands. Thanks to your nobles and leaders, the security of your forefathers has been squandered."

I let the impact of that statement sink in before continuing. "King Ahaz," I said, pointing, "will try to cut off the army of Cadrid before they reach Tira-Nor."

Wide-eyed faces stared at me from the eerie shadows cast by glowstone.

"But he will fail." I turned and faced the crowd. "And someone is going to have to do something about it."

King Ahaz rose and stepped forward. He cast a long shadow that draped across my face. "Fail?" he asked. "You claim now to know the future?"

"I saw blood on the north meadows," I answered. "And bodies falling like cut wheat."

"In that case," Ahaz said, "I think you must be allowed to live." He turned to the jury. "So that I can kill you myself when I return."

He stared at the jury, his eyes black, and then turned and swept out of the Great Hall in front of a long train of whispering nobles.

The prosecutor continued stroking his chin with his long fingers. "Which means we must keep you somewhere . . ." He stared at me as a wolf might gaze at a distant sheep. "Somewhere appropriate."

They bound my paws and carried me to a place both loathsome and familiar: PaTri's old storage room, now virtually empty.

It still reeked of maywort.

Chapter Twenty-Eight

Justice

The guards untied my bonds and tossed the cord in after me. I rubbed my wrists as they sealed the chamber with sticks, pebbles, and loose dirt, the light of the glowstones in the hall growing dimmer and dimmer as the opening gradually filled. At the last moment one of them flung in a handful of seeds and a lump of dried apple. Then they stuffed a stone into the crack near the ceiling and darkness crowded around me.

I don't know how long I lay there. It might have been hours, or even days.

At some point hunger awakened in my belly, and I groped my way over to the pile of debris and searched the floor with trembling fingers. I found the bit of apple by its smell. The seeds took longer to find, and helped only a little. They had not left me any water.

What had I been thinking? Why hadn't I tried to defend myself? Why had I allowed the kingsguard to haul me into Tira-Nor?

I leaned my head against the cool earth and closed my eyes, intending to bury myself in sleep.

Father's voice, from so far away it was almost inaudible, came like a distant sigh. *"They're coming, Son."*

I opened my eyes and immediately wished I hadn't.

Kalla entered through the wall just to my left, her great, flat head lowered, the black lids of her eyes rolling upward as she sidled to a pile of sticks stacked in one corner. A tiny army of beetles followed on her heels, clicking their jaw pincers and flowing over the earth in a black current.

Other creatures broke through the walls: a weasel, a rat, a mole, a white mouse with eyes as red as raspberries. A serpent the color of a maggot descended from the roof of the chamber in a long series of writhing thrusts, as though breaking free from a long bondage. Several nameless creatures I did not recognize appeared slowly near Kalla's tail, their misshapen black bodies swirling like fog-shadow, their faces empty and eyeless.

Their appearance nauseated me, but I felt no fear. Only that same sense of terrible reality and unfathomable power that had gripped me in Cadrid when I leapt into the river with Hammah.

More creatures arrived until the storage chamber swarmed with dark, flickering bodies. They spread out, encircling me. I kept to one edge and pressed my back against the wall, trying to shut out the unearthly sounds the lost souls made as they moved.

Kalla's great, black eyes rolled in her head, taking in the assembly gathered around her in two crescent lines like wings from her shoulders. "This trial," she said, "will come to order." Her voice dripped like cold water from the ceiling. "Who stands for the prosecution?"

"I do." The white mouse with red eyes rose almost weightlessly and strode to the center of the circle. "AaNoth the White." He gazed at me. In spite of myself, I averted my eyes.

"And who stands for the accused?" Kalla asked.

They gazed at me with cold stares that radiated hatred. I knew something was expected of me, but felt no obligation to give it.

"Who stands," Kalla asked again, her voice rising, "for the accused?"

AaNoth pointed. "He does. Eli, son of LiDel. Seer of Tira-Nor."

So I was a seer now, huh?

I pulled myself up straight and glared at them. "No," I said. "Whatever this is, I don't want any part of it. You're in my room and I'm sick of looking at you. Get out."

"This is not your room," AaNoth said. "We are here by invitation. You have no authority to remove us."

I started to protest, but sensed I was playing a high-stakes game, the rules of which had not yet been explained.

"Do you refuse to stand for the accused?" Kalla asked.

Accused. So it was to be another mockery of justice like the one I had just been through, but with fiends and freaks standing in the gallery. I did not want to give them the satisfaction of participating, but I didn't see any way out. Whatever they intended to do to me, they would do. At last I said, "What are the charges?"

AaNoth smiled cruelly and spoke to the gathered creatures. "Treachery," he said in a voice like an explosion. "Murder. Greed. Theft. Kidnapping." The lost souls in the circle grunted sounds of approval, their guttural cheers rising with AaNoth's voice as he spoke. "Every imaginable form of injustice and perversion."

The mole nodded his head and thumped the dirt floor with his front paws, grinning madly.

"I will prove these charges," AaNoth continued, "beyond all doubt. And when I am finished we shall agree that the defendant—" he looked at me, "—is worthy of death."

"Perversion?" I said. "This trial is the perversion. You have no evidence against me."

Kalla seemed to grin. Her lower jaw distended and a white tongue snaked out. "Against you?" she said. "Not yet, perhaps. But this trial is not about you."

AaNoth spread his paws in a gesture of helplessness and spoke again to the crowd. "Eli, son of LiDel, seems to suffer from a bloated ego. He thinks he is someone of consequence!"

The creatures cackled. They threw laughter at me as though it were filth from Dry Gully.

"Who then?" I shouted. "Who is on trial here?"

Kalla focused her black gaze on me. A shiver crept down my spine. "The accused," she said, "is the city of Tira-Nor. Will you stand for them?"

Silence fell. They stared at me with hungry eyes.

"You want me to defend them?" I asked. "Why should I?"

AaNoth held up one finger and chuckled lightly. "Indeed. Their crimes against you weigh heavily on my list."

I frowned, still puzzled. "If I refuse?"

"Then you refuse. There is no one else. Either way, justice shall be decided by this court."

Something about his statement didn't seem right. He looked so eager. "How can you determine justice," I asked, "if no one offers a defense?"

AaNoth shook his head. "You are the appointed seer of Tira-Nor and the only mouse qualified to stand on her behalf. If you will not defend her, she is not worth defending."

I looked from face to face. "If I'm the only mouse qualified to defend her," I asked, "what are you? What gives you the right to sit in judgment? Who made you lords over Tira-Nor?"

There was a short pause, followed by a collective outburst of laughter from the lost souls. "Us?" someone said. "Who made us lords?"

A moment later AaNoth held up one paw for silence. "I believe Eli, son of LiDel, already knows the answer to that question." He turned and gazed at me. "What do you think, Eli? Who made us the lords of Tira-Nor?"

A cold chill crept through my veins. I stood rooted to the floor as comprehension washed over me. "They did," I whispered. "Tira-Nor chose you."

AaNoth chuckled. "They did indeed," he said happily. "And whatever happens to them, they have it coming, as you well know. So tell us, Master Eli. Will you stand for the scum who left you here to rot? Or will you send them to the fate they deserve?"

Kalla's tongue flicked out, lingering in the air as though tasting a delicacy. "Will you stand for them? Of course not. And well you shouldn't. Why say a word on their behalf? Why move a whisker for those who would see you killed? No reason at all. A simple no will do. And we will leave you in peace."

AaNoth's face changed. His look grew passive, almost innocent. "You don't owe them anything."

Beetles clicked in expectancy. The weasel arched his back. The mole edged forward with what seemed like excitement.

AaNoth's eyes locked on mine. Though his face was a mask, he couldn't conceal the hatred for me that smoldered there, lit by the red-hot furnace of his soul. But that wasn't what decided me.

In that moment I remembered Father, and I knew what I must do because I knew what he would do.

I lifted my chin. "I'll stand for Tira-Nor," I said. "Even if she doesn't deserve it."

AaNoth's eyes flashed. Then he turned away and threw me an unconcerned shrug. "So be it. The verdict is inevitable anyway." He bowed to Kalla. "May I begin?"

Kalla nodded her great head once, and the black lids of her eyes rolled upward in a slow blink.

"Lords of Tira-Nor," AaNoth said, pacing slowly in the center of the circle. "This city is rotten to the core. Its leaders are corrupt, its citizens decadent. Every commoner defrauds his neighbor, and nobles sell their own servants into slavery out of spite. Kits are taken from nursing mothers, and every year at the Spring Festival the mice of Tira-Nor spill the blood of their kin for no better purpose than a few moments of entertainment!" The gallery cheered its approval, their faces twisted by strange, insatiable desires. Clearly they approved of these things, and yet they were eager to pass judgment.

"But their crimes are actually much worse than this," AaNoth continued, "because the mice of Tira-Nor ought to know better. They have the ancient stories! They have the seers and mice of valor." He shook his head and laughed slowly. "They have the Badger and the Owl. Ha ha ha ha!"

The gallery erupted again, this time with hoots and jeers. Several made strange gestures, the meaning of which I did not care to guess.

"Were Tira-Nor another Cadrid, another Leer, they might be accorded some measure of *mercy*." AaNoth said this last word as though it were distasteful, and someone made a gagging sound. "But it is not another Cadrid or Leer. Tira-Nor is the famous 'city of promise.' Chosen by ElShua himself," AaNoth continued in a mocking voice, eyes wide, mouth twisted into a weird grin, "to display his glo*oorrry*."

More boos. More mocking laughter.

"Eli, son of LiDel," Kalla said. The room fell silent again. "Do you deny the truth of these charges?"

I looked around at the cold, calculating faces. They were setting a trap for me, and I knew it. "You accuse them of much. But where is the evidence?"

AaNoth scoffed. He sidled up to me with an expression of utter disdain. "Is the evidence really in question?"

Out of spite, and perhaps because I did not like to be bullied, I said, "It is!"

AaNoth waved one paw and the mole slid forward. He spoke in a strange, mouselike voice: "Take the boy to the pens," the mole said. "He won't bring much. But then, I doubt PaTri really lost a month's supply of maywort."

An image, shaped by the vividness of Father's murder, formed itself in my mind. A kingsguard officer pointed at me, and a brute of a soldier threw me over his shoulder. I felt the pain of the moment only briefly, and then the mole's voice rang out again, this time indistinguishable from that of PaTri.

"If you had only kept your mouth shut and gone quietly to Cadrid, you might have met your mother there. Though of course she may not have survived her journey. The taskmasters were not so careful with their cargo back then. I remember her well. A thin, frail thing."

The weasel spoke, his voice mimicking mine: "You lie!"

"Do I?" The mole said in PaTri's voice. "What does it matter? Things have changed now. I have new plans for you. Queen IsaBel has authorized a special sacrifice for the Spring Festival. Guess who's invited?"

AaNoth grinned. "Or perhaps you remember this," he said, motioning to the beetles.

They formed a line and spoke, and their high, clicking voices somehow carried the exact timbre of the sentries who had celebrated my impending doom at the Spring Festival:

Here's to Kalla, quick and strong,
Who lends us speed to flee.
Life is short, and death is long.
Better him than me!

AaNoth held out his paws in a wide gesture, playing to the gallery. "If that fails to jog your memory, surely you cannot have forgotten this."

"I think you must be allowed to live," said the mole, though I might have sworn I heard King Ahaz. "So that I can kill you myself when I return."

When I did not answer, AaNoth pointed a finger at my chest. "You yourself called down curses on Tira-Nor! With your own mouth you cursed the king and queen. You cursed the nobles and the commoners, the kingsguard warriors, and the emissaries of Cadrid." He pursed his lips and stared at me. After a long silence he asked, in a voice of pure contempt, "Eli, son of LiDel, is the evidence really in question?"

"No," I said at last. "The charges are all true."

AaNoth's face lit with an unholy glee. "The defense speaks," he said. "He admits the city's guilt."

"But you are not weighing justice here," I protested. "Bad mice do not make a bad city. Just because some of them are thieves and murderers does not mean they all are. You can pile Tira-Nor's crimes all the way to the crest of Round Top, but you can't lay them all at the paws of each citizen."

AaNoth frowned as though trying to wrap his mind around my argument. "Do you mean to say," he said, "that we are accusing some of the mice of Tira-Nor without cause?"

"They're not all bad," I said. "They can't be. Surely there are a few who don't deserve to be lumped in with the rest."

AaNoth listened, his chin cupped in one paw, his eyes fixed on the ceiling. "I see," he said. "Somewhere, deep in the center of the whole rotten barrel, there is bound to be one good apple?"

One of the lost souls snorted in derision.

I ignored the sarcasm, my paws clenching into fists. "They aren't all bad!"

"All right," he said. "That's fair enough. What are their names?"

"I don't know their names," I said. "I know very few names. That doesn't mean they aren't there. Tira-Nor is a big city. Just because—"

"Of course!" he spat, his voice dripping condescension. "We can't expect someone like you, the seer of Tira-Nor, to actually know any good people."

The gallery laughed.

"You claim to be deciding justice. But nothing you claim against this city can be true so long as one good mouse lives here."

"No?" AaNoth's eyes gleamed like tiny flames in the darkness.

"It only takes one mouse," I said. Hope flickered in my chest. "One mouse to do something, somewhere. That's what Father believed. It always comes down to one mouse."

"I see," AaNoth said. He paced in front of me with his chin cupped in one paw. "But are you willing to stake your claim of Tira-Nor's innocence on such nonsense?"

"It isn't nonsense," I said through clenched teeth.

AaNoth waved away my objection. "Are you willing to abide by the judgment of this court if no good mouse can be found?"

"In all of Tira-Nor?" I asked, looking around at their hungry faces. "I am," I said. "As long as this court will find the city innocent for the sake of one good mouse!"

"Very well," AaNoth whispered. "Let us hear the evidence."

Too late my mind caught up to my mouth. Why were they so eager to make this wager? If they were really lords of Tira-Nor, why did they need me to abide by their judgment? What did they know that I didn't?

I opened my mouth to speak, but could think of nothing to say.

"When your father was murdered by King Ahaz and a squad of kingsguard soldiers," AaNoth said, "who came to his aid?"

I stared.

"Hmmm?" Obviously pleased with himself, he said, "No one? Well. But perhaps that's because they were frightened by the brutality of the occasionally bad mice of the kingsguard. Surely someone spoke out on your behalf after you were imprisoned?"

"How would I know that?"

"Of course you wouldn't. Very right of you to say so. We must all be very careful to stick to the evidence and not speculate about what might be. Just tell us the names of the mice who showed you some compassion while you lay on the floor of PaTri's storage chamber in excruciating pain." He pointed at my paw. "From a thorn driven through your flesh."

"There was an old mouse," I said. "He took the thorn out. He washed the wound."

AaNoth motioned to the mole, who spoke again, this time in the voice of the old mouse who had ripped the thorn from my paw: "You may untie his paws. In his condition he won't be walking anywhere soon. I imagine you'll have to carry him to the river when the time comes. Hold this."

"Oh, yes," AaNoth said. "Very good of him to keep you alive so PaTri could burn you to death at the Spring Festival. Is that your idea of innocence?"

I shook my head.

"So there you lay in PaTri's storage room, racked with infection and fever. Who else came to help you, hmmm? Who brought you a drink of cool water?"

"Mitts and Spew," I said without thinking.

"PaTri's acolytes?"

I nodded.

"Acting on orders?"

Again I nodded.

"Delivered, unless I'm mistaken, with frequent kicks to the face?"

I looked away. At one time I had wanted them to die. Now . . . "Are they still alive?" I asked.

AaNoth's brows came together. "The two mice who used to chase you? The ones who started all this by accusing you of spoiling maywort?"

"Yes," I said with determination. "Are they still alive?" For some reason I needed them to be.

"If they are," he said, "it is not because they have been good."

"This proves nothing," I said. "You haven't proven that all of Tira-Nor is bad."

AaNoth shrugged. "No," he agreed. "We've only proven that you've never met a good mouse in Tira-Nor. Nor a purple wombat, I suppose. And if one exists—"

"My Father!" I said. "My Father was a good mouse. And so was AlBaer. I knew them both!"

AaNoth raised his eyebrows. "Dead and dead," he said. He turned to face the gallery.

"Dead and dead," the lost souls repeated. "Dead and dead. Dead and dead. Dead and dead."

I glared at them as rage gathered in my chest. "Shut up!"

"Dead and dead and dead and dead."

AaNoth looked up at Kalla. "The prosecution rests."

Kalla's tongue shot out. "Eli, son of LiDel," she said. The noise of the gallery dribbled away into silence. "Have you anything to add?"

"Just this," I said. "If this trial really is some kind of justice, I don't want any part of it."

Kalla's great lizard eyes fixed on me for a long time as though looking through me to the wall. "Then why," she asked, "did you want so badly to lose?"

I stared at her as heat burned my face, then looked down. The scar on my paw burned white in the darkness. It was true. Part of me did want the city to suffer.

"The time of judgment has come," Kalla said. "Tira-Nor has violated the ancient laws. We find her guilty of crimes against herself, crimes against nature, crimes against ElShua. Tira-Nor must be judged. Because she has become like us, she must become one of us."

"Dead and dead," the gallery chanted.

"Tira-Nor shall be destroyed. Her citizens shall be enslaved, her nobles slaughtered on the fields of the North Meadows."

"Dead and dead!"

"Let this be the sentence written against the ancient city of promise." Kalla rose and nodded her flat, dripping head my direction. "By her own son shall Tira-Nor be enslaved.

"Eli, son of LiDel, Seer of Tira-Nor, you shall be her undoing!"

Chapter Twenty-Nine

Weak as Any Mouse

The mice of Leer came for him in the early morning.

Dawna shrieked at the entrance of RuHoff's cave.

Glyn woke with a start and rushed to the opening. He took one look at the dozens of white faces. "Back, whelps!" he roared, and launched himself into their midst. He struck one mouse on the jaw, a blow that should have crushed his skull.

The mouse only laughed. "Glyn the Weak!" he said.

The mice of Leer pinned Glyn to the ground and tied his limbs together. "Weak as any mouse!" they cheered.

Dawna watched from the cave entrance, her eyes wide, her mouth set in a firm line.

"Dawna?" Glyn asked, "What have you done?" The mice of Leer had not touched her. Besides, Glyn knew by her expression that she was responsible for whatever horrors awaited him.

At last she smiled. At last, at last. "Mashed raisins," she said. "In your breakfast. You didn't taste them?"

"I wondered what that was," he said. "But why?"

"You don't love me."

The mice of Leer hoisted him off the ground and carried him into the Dark Forest, where they gouged out his eyes with a sharp stick.

"I have a riddle for you!" a voice said. "What on earth is stronger than Glyn the Strong?"

Blood dribbled down Glyn's cheeks. Weakness such as he had never known trembled in his limbs. His body felt cold and lifeless. He wanted to die.

"Tell us!" other voices spat mockingly. "Tell us! Tell us!"

"A raisin!" the first voice said.

Then the mice of Leer carried Glyn back to their barn and tied him to a pole in the center. Day after day, from early morning until late at night, they cuffed his cheeks and asked him silly, pointless riddles with no good answer.

And every day they offered him raisins, though they never gave him any. Whatever raisins they found, they kept to themselves.

Chapter Thirty

The Hall of Revelation

Something thumped the back of my head. Stone and bits of dirt rattled down the wall.

Light pierced the darkness. Paws dug at the mounded debris, widening the hole near the ceiling.

A glowstone, held aloft by an older mouse with gray whiskers, appeared through the hole next to his face. "Master Eli," he said. "Are you all right?"

All right? I blinked. Someone wanted to know if I was all right? "Thirsty," I said.

He backed out of the hole, and a moment later a huge chunk of apple sailed through to my feet. I devoured it as he widened the hole and then crawled through the opening on his belly.

He kneeled before me in the dirt. "Master Eli, we need your help."

It was such a simple statement, and yet I didn't understand what he meant. "My help?"

"You were right," he said. "King Ahaz led the kingsguard and militia to the North Meadows."

"And?"

"They're all dead."

"What about Queen IsaBel?"

"Still in the palace, protected by her personal guard." He shook his head. "But we are told she sent a messenger to the Cadridian general."

"What message?"

"We don't know. But no messengers have been seen going in through the Royal Gate. KoTsu's army is regrouping in the North Meadows. They had scattered everywhere, chasing remnants of the kingsguard."

My paws shook, though whether from hunger or fear I couldn't tell. "Who is 'we'?"

He looked back at the hole. "The mice of the Commons. What's left of the militia. A few of the lesser nobles who have no love for the queen."

"Why are you telling me this?"

"Our army is lost, Eli. Our king is dead. Some of us think we need a different sort of help now. The sort AlBaer would have given if—" His voice trailed away.

"AlBaer," I said. "Yes. But I'm not him."

He looked down for a long moment. "After the way we treated you, I wouldn't blame you if you spat in my face. But—" He lifted his chin and stared at me, his eyes as black as deep water. "—There isn't anyone else. You're the only seer we have."

The only seer.

I stared at him as his words gnawed a hole in the back of my mind. Had I learned anything from AlBaer? He certainly hadn't taught me to level armies, or to call forth fire from water. My apprenticeship had lasted less than a day. I'd been enslaved in Cadrid and imprisoned in Tira-Nor. I'd wasted my time with AlBaer complaining and looking at the wrong—

"Eli will deliver your message," AlBaer said to Hammah again in my mind, interrupting me. *"It is our duty. Regardless of the fate that awaits us."*

Was that all it meant to be a seer? Carrying messages?

I may not have learned to control AlBaer's powers, but I did have his words. I had an order from Surrah Hammah to General KoTsu. But would that be enough?

"What's your name?" I asked.

"Reese. Colonel Reese. Over the militia."

I rose slowly on trembling limbs, feeling very hollow. "What do you think of justice, Colonel Reese?" I asked.

He considered the question for a long time. "I guess that depends which side of it I'm standing on."

I smiled. "Me too," I said. I padded slowly over to the hole. "Any idea how much time we have before KoTsu arrives?"

He scratched his jaw with hooked fingers. "A day. Maybe two."

"All right. I'll do what I can. Make sure your sentries don't let anyone else leave Tira-Nor. And can you get me some more food?"

"Where are you going?"
"RuHoff's cave."

◆ ◆ ◆

The corridors leading into the North Gate complex were graveyard quiet. The sentries standing watch there—two adolescent males with no obvious kingsguard training—grew silent as I approached. They wouldn't look me in the eye, and I passed unchallenged into sunlight and a brisk wind.

I jogged north until the gate was out of sight, checking Round Top over one shoulder every few moments. Grayfeather was nowhere to be seen.

Evening approached, and I considered the likelihood of General KoTsu believing that Hammah had called off his attack. Why should he believe me? It didn't make sense. *I* wouldn't believe me.

I ran northeast and eventually looked down on the fields of the North Meadows. Grass hid most of the carnage, but grisly hints of blood and death surfaced here and there. Faces. Bodies. Tracks of crimson that trailed off into shadow.

KoTsu's army would take cover in the trees until most of the stragglers had returned. His army would be at the gates of Tira-Nor no later than tomorrow afternoon, possibly sooner.

AlBaer hadn't prepared me for any of this. What had he been thinking?

I glanced over one shoulder and then looked back at the field. It lay exactly as I had seen it in my vision the day King Ahaz had arrested me.

I closed my eyes and tried to imagine what AlBaer would do were he here. The next moment I noticed what I was doing, and shook my head. I used to wonder what Glyn might do in my place. Now I wondered what AlBaer would do. And I didn't even like AlBaer.

AlBaer—who had made me run to Cadrid, and then walked to Cadrid not in a day, or even an hour, but in a single step. AlBaer—who destroyed PaTri and his acolytes. AlBaer—who pitied his enemies and tortured his friends.

It occurred to me that it didn't really matter what AlBaer would have done in my place, because AlBaer wasn't here. Besides, I would never be able to re-create his miracles. He hadn't shown me how to do anything.

"He showed you how to run like Glyn the Strong," Father's voice whispered in my ear.

"Different," I said. "He was standing right there next to me."

"He said you didn't need him any more."

"He was wrong."

"Oh?"

"I don't know anything, don't have any power, don't—"

"You have whatever AlBaer had."

I turned away from the field and fled southwest, away from Father's voice, toward RuHoff's cave.

Father's voice followed me, as persistent as a cat. *"AlBaer said so himself. 'Whatever was mine is yours.' "*

"He was talking about his stuff!" I shouted to the wind. "The cave, the . . . the . . . you know. . . the straw pallet!" I stopped in the grass, panting, and stuck my fingers in my ears to keep Father's voice outside my head. "I'm not Glyn," I said. "I'm not RuHoff. I'm not AlBaer."

"No," Father said. His voice slipped under my fingers. *"You are Eli!"*

I shook my head and pressed my eyes shut. "No," I said. "I'm not! I'm not even Eli! I wear disguises. I'm not myself. I'm never myself. And if I were myself, I wouldn't know it. I don't know who I am!"

Father whispered once more, calm and certain and full of quiet confidence. A hint of laughter tinged the edges of his voice. *"You are Eli, son of LiDel. Seer of Tira-Nor, advisor to the king, and voice of ElShua in the Known Lands."*

◆ ◆ ◆

The sun hung low on the horizon as I dropped over the top of the rock and scratched at the cave entrance. A habit, of course. I knew no one would be there.

Inside, AlBaer's pallet lay in a disorderly pile, just as I had left it. A rush of guilt flooded through me. I had kicked his straw out of spite, and then he disappeared. Why should that make me ashamed, when I had done far worse without feeling any quiver of remorse?

I scooped the straw pallet up and remade it, more or less as it had been yesterday, then turned as though in a dream and stared at the crack in the corner.

I had known all along what I meant to do, but I did not let myself think about it. I was afraid that if I thought about it I would not believe, and that would ruin everything.

In the corner I stooped and pressed one paw to the crack that ran floor to ceiling. I closed my eyes and pictured AlBaer on the other side of the crack. "You made me your apprentice," I said. "You owe me."

He laughed, his eyes twinkling. "In order to see," he said, "one must understand the curse of the seer. Do you, Eli? Do you understand the curse of the seer?"

I nodded. It was no riddle he asked me. I had been learning the truth of the answer since the day Father died. "It's not something you pronounce," I said. "It's something you endure. The curse of the seer is loneliness."

AlBaer stepped aside, and I pushed into the crack, wriggling against the cold, saw-blade edges. The stone wall groaned and split apart as I pushed inward. Jagged slabs of rock moved aside—reluctantly, it seemed to me, though my shoulders were not so wide as Glyn's.

Then the roof opened up and the floor dropped away, and I stood in a dark, narrow passage.

In the distance a yellow beam of light slit the passageway at an angle, coming down from a crack in the rock high above. I followed the light down a hall cased in stone and sheathed in dust. Night would fall soon, and the light would surely vanish. But in that place I felt as though I might live forever, that the sun would never set, that I had nothing to fear. I felt as though I had left all worries and all pretense—indeed, the greater part of myself—back in the cave, and yet was more myself for the loss.

The masks, I thought. That's what I left outside. All the faces that weren't really mine anyway.

The hall ended at blank rock. High on the wall to my right, Glyn's etchings were visible as a single island of scribbles caked in dust.

It was true. He had really come here. He had really carved the stone with just a fingernail.

I reached up with one paw and touched the smooth, gray surface. "ElShua," I said, "I'm sorry I am not Glyn, or RuHoff, or even AlBaer. But I am not them, and never will be. I am only myself. Eli, son of LiDel, of the Commons."

I could not have carved anything into the rock even if I had dared. Instead, just underneath Glyn's "I do not want to be strong any more," I traced my sentence in the dust with the tip of one nail.

I wrote:

I am small.

The sound of a single finger polishing stone startled me. I turned. Fear flooded through my body, along with a power like a thousand bees humming in a hive.

The Ghost Badger's face flickered before me and disappeared.

On the opposite wall, in letters larger than my body, he had written three words in the dust:

You are strong!

Chapter Thirty-One

Blinding Faith

I left the cave hours before sunrise and headed east.

Shapes followed at my heels. Most of them crept along in the shadows of trees and stands of tall grass. A heavy moon sailed the black, cloudless waters overhead, shedding light on the blue-green fields north of Tira-Nor. When a lost soul stepped into moonlight, its body dissolved into a translucent gray mist, flickering half-formed and yet still visible, mirroring my movements.

Worse, another shape moved in the pale light beyond them. It too seemed to waver and reform as it slithered up through the grass at the bottom of the slope. It moved methodically, weaving, splitting itself around a rock and reforming on the other side, widening and narrowing its body as it moved.

KoTsu's army.

I crested the slope just north of Tira-Nor and turned to face all of them. With the moon behind me I would be clearly visible to their sentries.

AaNoth bounded up the slope, though his paws did not seem to really touch the earth. He stood at my side, his red eyes burning in the cool air.

"What do you want?" I asked.

"I wouldn't miss this for anything." He pointed at the mice in the distance. "Judgment has come. At last Tira-Nor will get what she deserves."

"Judgment? What makes you think I'm here to bring about your vision of judgment?"

"My vision?" He rubbed his paws together, grinning maliciously. "Not mine. Yours. You are the seer of Tira-Nor. You're the one who was wronged. Judgment will come from your lips."

"I don't want judgment."

"Oh, ho!" he said. "Then you want chaos! That will serve its purpose too."

I strained at the air with my nose. The night seemed charged. Power flowed through my limbs in bursts, growing and fading like the song of a cicada. "Chaos? No."

"The laws have not been broken," he said. "They have been shattered. You know it's true. Tira-Nor deserves to die. And you, Seer, cannot have it both ways. If the laws are not enforced, they are meaningless."

I looked over one shoulder toward the city. No gates were visible at this distance, but I knew where they lay. I imagined sentries gathered in the mouth of the Royal Gate, waiting for the inevitable.

AaNoth's voice suddenly took on a warm, sympathetic quality. Almost musical. He looked down. "King Ahaz is dead. And the kingsguard. Judgment begins at the top. But there is another who shouldn't live. Who mustn't live. For the sake of the city."

Yes. Though I did not trust him, his words made sense. "IsaBel."

He nodded slowly, made a little grunt in the back of his throat. "Her black deeds would darken the moon, were they spread like paper across the sky."

At some point in the hall of revelation—I don't know exactly when—I had stopped hating her. I had stopped thinking about her. But AaNoth was right. She mustn't be allowed to poison Tira-Nor further.

"IsaBel deserves to die," I said.

"We are agreed then." AaNoth's form wavered, barely visible.

KoTsu's advance scouts spotted me and pointed, sniffing the wind for some sign of other mice.

I straightened my back and stood in full silhouette at the crest of the hill.

One of the scouts turned and disappeared.

"But what of Cadrid?" AaNoth asked. "What about her deeds?"

"What of them?"

He sucked his teeth. "Justice." He pointed down the hill, then swept his paw in a semicircle toward Tira-Nor. "You have a perfect opportunity. A chance to see justice done. Judgment must come to all of them. Cadrid and Tira-Nor both."

"That's not my mission," I said.

"It is your mission! You are the voice of ElShua in the Known Lands! Do you deny the horrors of the warehouse, the cedar mill, the death-squads?"

I shook my head.

"What of Newbie, crushed to death by a jar of peanut cream to suit the delicate taste of Cadrid's nobles? What of the mice of Tira-Nor who labor there still? Do you really believe Hammah will long keep his slaves idle?"

Hammah break his promise? Why not? Cadrid depended on slaves. It was childish to think a king could remake a whole society and culture, an economy and a way of thinking, based on a whim.

"They dream of freedom still," AaNoth said.

Below me, a ring of Cadridian warriors approached slowly, looking from side to side as though expecting a trap.

"You have the power," AaNoth said, smiling. "I can see it in you, coursing through your veins."

He spoke truth. The current of the world between pulsed and flickered under my skin, growing in intensity like a storm on the horizon.

"Pull the power toward you," he said. "Gather it in your fists." He closed his eyes, lifted his snout, took a long pull of the night air. "Gather it in your lungs, your belly, your chest."

"Ho there!" A Cadridian soldier said.

I held up one paw, palm out. The advancing Cadridian soldiers stopped. "Send for General KoTsu," I said.

Something like puzzlement flickered across their faces. One of them turned and sped away, probably not knowing why he did so.

But I knew. My commands were not to be disregarded.

AaNoth leaned in close. His voice came as a whisper. "Wait until they have gathered around you. Then say the word, and judgment will be unleashed!"

The word. It came unbidden into my mind, glowing like a spark tossed from a fire. Power came with it, and the certainty of its effect. I had not known a killing word existed until that moment. But suddenly the full power and meaning of the word struck my mind like a clenched fist. I knew—*knew!*—that this word would rend flesh and crack bones.

Ginnosh!

AaNoth smiled knowingly. "It is an ancient word," he said, as though he could see the word floating there in my mind. "Very ancient. It means—"

"Judgment," I said. Power flooded through me, offered itself to me— mine to dispel, to channel, to use or misuse as I chose.

He nodded once, his eyes slits. "Cadrid deserves to die."

I considered this. "Yes."

"You can make things right. Pay them back."

Was that the solution? One word? One simple display of power to crush Tira-Nor's enemies?

"That power," AaNoth said, "the power you feel right now—"

"—Comes from ElShua," I said.

He winced at the name. "It does. And it is for this purpose. You must make things right. Your father said—"

I snapped my head around to look at him. "My father?"

He stared into my eyes as though searching for something. A look of uncertain fury flashed across his face. "Your father said it always comes down to one mouse. That's you."

"And if I destroy KoTsu's army now, how will I bring judgment to Tira-Nor?"

AaNoth smiled.

Images pressed themselves into my mind. Thoughts and plans formed a tapestry of action more powerful than any fable told by light of glowstone in the Great Hall, a plan so powerful and perfect I could almost smell the smoke from the fires of destruction.

I closed my eyes and let the waves wash over me. Cadrid deserved to die, so I would level her army. I would leave one mouse alive to return to Cadrid with the story and ensure Cadrid stayed away forever.

Then I would turn to Tira-Nor and empty the palace. IsaBel would die. The palace guard would die, for they knew what she was and still protected her.

The Greater Families would be leveled. The Lesser Families would be left somewhat intact, with one in four surviving to manage the city. The Commons . . .

Memories floated before me. Mice ducking into their chamber holes as the kingsguard beat my father, jabbed his throat, left him in a lifeless huddle outside our home.

The Commons too would be punished, but not destroyed. One in three would live.

Judgment. Justice. A permanent righting of the world.

The power lay within my grasp. Tira-Nor deserved to suffer.

A thought whispered from a dark corner of my mind, pointing at the word *Ginnosh* like a child who has found something long lost.

Except . . .

Was that really what I wanted?

Was that really why I'd come?

I opened my eyes. "The army of Cadrid will die?"

"Yes."

"And most of Tira-Nor?"

He sniffed. "As you say."

"That part bothers me," I said. "Why only *most* of Tira-Nor, when you said there was not one good mouse left in the whole city?"

AaNoth blinked, wavering in the moonlight. He pressed his lips together.

"Why not destroy all of it?" I asked. "Why should any of them live?"

He pointed a finger at my chest. "You're no seer if you cannot pronounce judgment."

Truth broke over me like a thunderclap. *Ginnosh* was a trap. The killing word was just that. Killing. It would not end at the ranks of KoTsu's army. It would spread across the meadows and strike at the heart of Tira-Nor the moment it left my lips.

The Cadridians would die, the mice of Tira-Nor would die, I would probably die too. There would be no one left. *Ginnosh* was a genie that, once set free, could not be forced back into its bottle.

"I never wanted to be a seer," I said.

A sound like water sloshing from a trough forced my gaze downhill. Mice advanced in a wave up the slope before me, bending the grass in a crooked line. Before them, an older mouse with a splotch of brown fur that draped his shoulders strode effortlessly into the moonlight.

"You have asked for General KoTsu," he said. "And here shall I be."

Splotch. Hammah's general. His eyes widened in recognition. "Twopence!"

I nodded. "King Ahaz is dead?"

"Yes," he said simply. "As are most of your kingsguard warriors."

"Cadrid lost twenty-three priests. Tira-Nor has lost hundreds. Is our debt not paid?"

"That is not for my deciding," he said. "You shall go now. Away from Tira-Nor."

I shook my head. "I have a message for you from Surrah Hammah. He commands you to leave Tira-Nor unharmed and returned to Cadrid."

His eyes narrowed. "How shall you know this?"

"I heard him speak the words to AlBaer."

"And where is the seer?"

I glanced up into the sky. "Gone."

I barely saw the shadow entered his head. It slid into his mouth in a flash of dripping black, a flicker of movement caught only in the corner of my eye. I thought, *Kalla would counsel both of us!* And I knew before he spoke what he was going to say.

He gave a long sigh. "I shall not take the words of a slave over the words of Surrah Hammah!"

I stretched my hands out, pleading. "King Ahaz dishonored you, and he has paid for it with many souls, including his own. What else would you have from us?"

"I take Tira-Nor for Surrah Hammah. Dead or alive shall make no difference."

"And what of justice?" I asked. "Does that make a difference?"

"We do not fight for justice," KoTsu answered, "but for honor."

I took a deep breath. "I am the seer of Tira-Nor. AlBaer has passed, and his power has fallen to me. I would have you leave peacefully."

KoTsu seemed to consider this, which surprised me. I expected him to dismiss me without a second thought. "I too would have us leave peacefully," he said. "But that choice is not mine to make."

"I'm sorry then," I said.

KoTsu nodded to a mouse at his right elbow. "Kill him."

AaNoth's shadow flickered, and a cold chill crept through my bones. "Now," he said. "The word! Or it will be too late for any of you."

Mice sprang forward.

I closed my eyes, sucked in the roar of energy around me, and let it flow from my tongue in a single violent burst: *"Kuh'lech!"*

Light burst in front of me like a thousand suns, painting my eyelids a brilliant white as hard and as smooth as marble. A crack louder than lightning split the sky. Fire hung before me in a ball so close I could almost touch it. I saw it with the clarity of morning through my closed eyelids.

Coils of light shot through the air, forking from skull to skull, stabbing the eyes of the Cadridians and splintering into thousands of twisting beams.

Wind burst from my mouth in a gale, knocking the soldiers to their knees and pressing their heads down to the turf even as it streaked their fur.

The fire disappeared.

Beside me, AaNoth shook. "*Kuh'lech*?" he hissed. "What is *kuh'lech*?!" Fury chiseled his voice.

"Something you do not understand," I said. "And never will. It is an ancient word. As old as *ginnosh*." I don't know how I knew this, but the knowledge was there in my mind as though I had been born with it. "It means mercy."

The mice of Cadrid made sounds. Small sounds. Whimpers. Groans. Mewls. A few put out one paw, as though feeling their way over uneven ground. Most lay motionless where they had fallen.

I stepped forward and reached down to General KoTsu, put one paw on his back.

He flinched. "Who are you?" he asked.

"Eli. Seer of Tira-Nor."

"What have you done to me?"

"Not just you," I said. "Your whole army. I have taken your sight."

His body stiffened. "Better to have killed us."

"Why?"

"A mouse who cannot see is no mouse at all."

"Then you have never been a mouse." I leaned closer and whispered in his ear. "Would you have your eyes back? Even from one such as me?"

He lifted his head, then nodded slowly.

"Let this be the sentence written against the ancient city of promise," said a voice like cracking ice in my ear. Startled, I turned in time to see Kalla's great, shimmering mouth split into a wide, terrifying grin. "Eli, son of LiDel, seer of Tira-Nor, you shall be her undoing!"

A feeling of cold dread crept over me. She spoke as if she knew something I didn't. And she was probably right. How much did I really know about my own city?

I was about to risk everything on the hope of finding something that probably didn't exist: one good mouse in all of Tira-Nor.

If I was wrong, I would be helpless, a tool of the lost souls, and the cause of Tira-Nor's destruction.

I shrugged the thought aside and tapped General KoTsu's shoulder. "Order your mice to make a single line, nose to tail," I said. "Then take my paw. I will lead you back to seeing."

Chapter Thirty-Two

Blind Sacrifice

When autumn came, it carried to Glyn the smell of apples, the rustle of dry leaves, and the cool tang of frost in the morning.

He felt the sun on his face for a few hours each evening as it arced through a window in the side of the barn. Its buttery warmth slid farther down his left cheek now that the days grew shorter and its zenith closer to the sill.

The mice of Leer still taunted him daily, but now they quickly tired of tormenting him and generally left him alone. Glyn's wrists were swollen and encrusted with blood from where the bonds sliced into his flesh, but they did not care to loosen his bonds.

Autumn also brought Dawna back to her father's home in the barn. She stood at a distance and stared at Glyn for a long time.

Glyn knew her by her scent. "Hello, Dawna," he said.

She moved to walk past him.

"I'm sorry," Glyn said, "for not loving you."

"You're sorry?" She grabbed a fistful of straw from the barn floor, took a step nearer Glyn, but then threw it down again. "Hmph!"

"Do you know what is wiser than a question asked in the dark?" he asked.

"Shut up," she said.

He nodded.

"Shut up," she said again. "I don't care what's wiser. Just shut up." Then she stomped away, reminding herself how much he had wronged her. She had thought seeing Glyn suffer for his arrogance and cruelty to her and her family would fill her emptiness. And yet….

"Nothing," Glyn said after the sound of her steps faded. "Nothing is wiser than a question asked in the dark."

He turned his face toward the sun and said, "ElShua, I have become small. Surely, no mouse has ever been smaller. And I am in darkness, so at last I have a chance to be wise. Will you make me strong again, for just one moment?"

In the distance, a lone cicada wheezed out its forlorn song like someone late for a party. In the barn, not a soul moved. Glyn could not even hear the steps of sentries at the barn doors. Everything had gone still and silent under a blanket of overpowering heat.

Something like ice water splashed over his arms, cold and bracing and wonderful. It wrapped itself around his wrists and hardened into a steely ring against his flesh. The red *whump-whump-whump* of pain that had been throbbing up his arms for weeks died.

His toes tingled. His nose twitched. Every whisker vibrated with unseen power. He stood slowly, his back to the post in the center of the barn.

Snap! The cord binding one wrist fell to the floor. *Snap*! The other wrist came free.

Glyn shook himself like a hound, lifted his nose, and felt for the rough wood texture of the pole.

"Listen, you!" someone said. "Sit back down—"

Behind him, a mouse screamed. Voices rang out in the warm air, joining like strands of wire. Fear, hatred, panic. From their holes, the mice of Leer converged on the barn as though summoned.

The barn hummed with the motion and chatter of mice responding to an emergency they did not understand. At first, only a few even noticed Glyn. So many mice crowded the barn that most of them only noticed each other. Each of them looked for an obvious explanation of the warning cry. Then someone hopped to a rotting hay bale and said, "Look! The Glyn!"

They all looked.

For a moment he did nothing. He had a choice to make. He was *himself* again. Finally himself. He could feel it.

But did he want to be? He had just this one moment to decide his future. Was he strong enough to be Glyn the Wise? Or weak enough to be Glyn the Strong?

"Someone untied him!" a mouse shouted. "Quick! Bring him down!"

Glyn drew himself up and took a deep breath. He spread his hind legs wide for support. He took the post in his front paws and hugged it tight to his chest.

The mice of Leer hesitated. Something about the way he stood told them he was not the same Glyn they had been tormenting. Mouse looked to mouse. Who would be first? Where are the sentries? This isn't my responsibility!

At last the mouse on the hay bale leapt down, shrieking his war challenge and bounding toward Glyn with bared teeth.

I am strong!

Glyn jammed his paws against the post and lifted.

The barn shuddered. Mice pointed, shrieked, and fled for the nearest hole. The center post tried to say no, but at last shrugged and gave in, along with the ceiling, loft, and three of the four walls. The fourth wall leaned against the mound of debris that had once been the barn. Weathered gray wood lay in a pile like the bones of a long-dead animal, belching dust in a cloud the shape of a baker's hat.

For a long time silence ruled the yard. Then, somewhere far off, the cicada wheezed out its lonely song once more.

◆ ◆ ◆

When the mice of Tira-Nor heard about the destruction of Leer and the death of Glyn the Strong, they sent a delegation of warriors from the kingsguard to retrieve his body. But though they crawled among the dusty, cracking wood for two days, they never found it.

They did find something. In the hole where the center post once stood, they found a cord of braided sawgrass.

Chapter Thirty-Three

Evidence

Sunrise lit the fields above Tira-Nor by the time we arrived. Outside the Royal Gate I stopped the trudging, bewildered Cadridians and split them into dozens of smaller lines, then led them forward into even rows. Guards from the palace gathered in a knot at the gate hole while I worked. They stared out of the blackness and said not a word.

When I had finished, KoTsu's army formed a rectangular mass of silent, groping mice, each still clutching the tail of the mouse in front of him. The first row of mice looked particularly terrified.

Colonel Reese had stationed two dozen militia mice outside the Royal Gate to prevent IsaBel sending messengers to KoTsu. These mice retreated back up the slope to the larger entry hole of North Gate. Like the palace guard, they watched as I formed the Cadridians into a mass at Tira-Nor's doorstep.

Sounds swept around me in a current, but I knew no one else heard them. Beetles clicked in the grass all around us. A mole made little humming noises through his nose. Water dripped from webbed feet. I almost felt the cold fingers of the lost souls wrapping around my neck.

I turned and faced the Royal Gate. "Captain!" I said to the commander of the palace guard, knowing he would be listening. "Bring Queen IsaBel."

A mouse, stiff as cardboard, emerged into sunlight. "I am Captain DeVree," he said. "I will carry whatever message you have to the queen."

"Captain DeVree," I said, nodding in a kind of informal salute, "I do not have a *message* for the queen. I gave a *command* concerning the queen. Bring her out!"

His gaze fanned KoTsu's army, then returned to my face. "Command? Who are you?"

I drew myself up to my full, unimposing height. "I am Eli, son of LiDel, former apprentice to AlBaer and now seer of Tira-Nor."

He scowled at me for a long time, then nodded back toward the palace. "I can ask, but she won't come."

"I did not say that you should ask," I said. I plucked a few blades of grass from the earth and cast them to the breeze. "I said that you should bring her."

A smile tugged at his mouth, as though he would have liked nothing better but knew I wasn't serious. "What do you really want?"

"How do you expect this to end, Captain?"

He glanced behind me for just a moment. "What do you mean?"

"King Ahaz is dead. The kingsguard is gone. The militia is against you. General KoTsu—" I jabbed a thumb over one shoulder, "—knows how to get around the wall stones. How long do you think you can hold out against them?"

He stuck his chin out. "As long as we need to."

Which was either a lie or wishful thinking. "So you're an optimist," I said.

"Better than a traitor." He nodded in the direction of the Cadridians.

I turned and looked at them. He couldn't know they were blind, though surely he noticed something amiss in the way they stood, the way they stared without blinking. "You misunderstand, Captain. Whether or not Tira-Nor is destroyed is not up to me. Will you bring the queen?"

He stared at me unblinking, then disappeared into the gate hole.

I looked over my shoulder at General KoTsu, who was staring blankly at the sky above the horizon. "General," I said, "wait here a moment."

I turned to my left and strode toward the mouth of the North Gate, slightly higher up and farther away, but still visible in the morning sunlight. "Colonel Reese!"

Reese emerged from the shadowy entrance and plodded a few steps down the slope, his gaze fixed on the ranks of Cadridians behind me. "Master Eli?"

I stopped midway between the Cadridian army and the gate. "Do you trust me, Colonel?"

He glanced toward the Royal Gate, then back at the gathered troops. "Is that a trick question?"

I grinned. "Call out the militia," I said. "Bring them out here. Tell them to form ranks. Then meet me here on the slope."

He frowned. "We'll be outnumbered." He looked again at the motionless ranks of Cadridian warriors. "Ten to one."

I did not tell him the number was more like twenty to one, not even including the lost souls, who wanted all of us dead. "Yes," I said. "But do it anyway?"

He hesitated just a moment, then turned and loped back to the gate.

It took several minutes for the mice of the militia to begin spilling from the gate hole. At first they huddled together in a widening knot above us on the field, shaking with fear and anticipation as they caught a glimpse of KoTsu's army. Newly appointed officers shouted orders in high, uncertain voices that drifted on the breeze. The air grew heavy, pregnant with something like rain, though the sky radiated a blue as cloudless as sapphire.

When the militia finally stood in ragged lines on the high ground of the meadow, Colonel Reese plodded slowly down the slope, like someone going to a certain death. He stopped in front of me, his face the color of ash. "It is done," he said. "Now what?"

I took a deep breath. “Now,” I said, “We have a trial.”

For the first time that morning he tore his gaze off the Cadridians and looked me full in the face. “I don’t understand.”

The earth around him moved, but he did not notice it. Grass shuddered in a wave, dimpling and reforming like lava struck by a giant fist. Behind him a dark head rose from the soil, shimmering black and green, translucent in the warm glow of the sun.

Kalla shook her head, spraying an arc of water as black as oil into the air. Some of the drops went through Reese’s body, but he didn’t notice this either. He couldn’t see her, couldn’t hear her, so I kept my gaze forward.

“The mice of Cadrid are blind,” I said.

Reese glanced at KoTsu’s army, confusion wrinkling his nose. “What do you mean?”

“I mean they can’t see anything right now. The sunrise you’re looking at is nothing but black to them.”

His eyes widened. “How?”

“Does it matter?”

“Since you brought them here, I’d say it matters very much.”

“All right,” I said. “Do you remember what AlBaer did to the priests at the Spring Festival?”

He nodded.

Behind him, Kalla lifted her grotesque body from the earth and plodded all four limbs onto the surface. Her tail whipped in a wide semicircle.

“It was something a lot like that,” I said, “only no one died.”

"You did this?"

I shrugged. "Yes."

"Why?"

"So I could bring them here to you."

"For a trial?"

"Yes."

Behind him, Kalla laughed. Her voice was cold and wheezing and humorless. "You won't win this," she gurgled. "This mouse is already mine."

I ignored her and pointed up the slope. "Your militia is no match for them in a fair fight. But now I suppose you could slaughter them easily enough. I don't think KoTsu's mice want to live any more."

Colonel Reese shook his head slowly. "I still don't understand why you brought them here."

"I brought them here for you, Colonel. You will decide their fate. After you hear the evidence against them."

"Why me?"

"Because . . ." I said. And I thought, *Because you know right from wrong, even if you don't always do it. Because it always comes down to one mouse, and someone has to be that mouse. Because when I look at you I see my father*. But I said none of these things. Instead, I said, "Because you are in command." Which was true enough.

He lifted his chin and stared down at the Cadridian troops. "Very well. Let's hear it."

I turned and stood looking downhill, away from Kalla's shimmering hide and black, empty eyes. "The Cadridians are a merciless people, with no respect for the young, no respect for the old, no respect for females or kits or the dying. They spend their days feasting on peanut cream purchased with the lives of our friends and loved ones. But they don't enjoy it, even for a moment. They are too lost in their own hopelessness to take any notice of the suffering of others. They have built their empire on blood and death, and now they serve both so readily that they have forgotten even why they make war on other colonies. They capture and kill because they hate life, even in themselves."

Colonel Reese stroked his chin with one paw as he listened, his gaze never wavering.

"And so they have marched against Tira-Nor to destroy the city and enslave its people. They destroyed most of the kingsguard. I saw the blood and the bodies, and General KoTsu does not deny it. He carries orders to show us no mercy. In fact, I made him an offer of peace a few hours ago. He responded by ordering his soldiers to kill me."

Reese still stroked his chin with one paw.

Kalla leaned her head down beside Reese's. Her mouth was next to his ear, but she was looking at me. "Cadrid would kill all of us without remorse."

I shot Kalla a look of disgust. *I don't need your help!*

"Say it," she whispered. "Say it or this trial is a sham, and you cannot win."

I glared at her.

"Cadrid," she breathed, "would kill all of us without remorse."

I looked back to Reese. "Cadrid would kill all of us without remorse."

"They deserve to die," Kalla whispered.

"They deserve to die."

Her mouth twitched. "They killed TuRue."

I looked into her eyes. *TuRue? Who is TuRue?*

"Say it!" Her voice came with a sound like the wind breaking itself to pieces against barren trees.

It won't matter, I thought at her, though I knew it would.

"Say it!"

"And," I said softly, "they killed TuRue."

Reese's eyes flashed. He made a fist with one paw. "You saw this?"

I shook my head. "I just know."

He nodded and stared down at the Cadridians with a cold, calculating expression. "I told him to stay out of the kingsguard."

"I'm sorry."

"Is there anything else I should know?"

I shrugged. "I could go on, but why bother? You've heard enough."

"Yes," he said. "I have."

"And?"

He lifted his head and took a deep breath, oblivious to Kalla's presence beside him. "And they don't deserve to live."

Kalla smiled.

Chapter Thirty-Four

Seers

I stood staring into the dirt as a nauseating sense of despair crawled into my stomach and took up residence. What had I done? Why had I brought the Cadridians to Tira-Nor? I should have led them back to Cadrid! That moment, the moment of blindness, I had not just taken sight from KoTsu's army. I had taken it from myself.

Reese would give the order. Of course he would. A few months ago I would have given the order. And why not? The mice of Cadrid did deserve to die.

And Tira-Nor would gain a few months of peace. Long enough for Cadrid to raise another army. Or the Leerians, perhaps, hearing of the decimation of the kingsguard, would send a Death Legion.

It wouldn't matter. All possibilities ended the same way. The battle of this moment was the only battle that mattered. And I had lost. Tira-Nor did belong to the lost souls. Because she was like them, Tira-Nor would become one of them.

Colonel Reese cleared his throat. "I'm just wondering—"

I looked up. "Yes?"

"What do you want me to do?"

I shook my head. "You are the judge, not me."

"I'm not their judge," he said. "Who made me a judge?"

A spark of hope began to glow in the back of my mind. "Every mouse is a judge. And every sneer is a guilty verdict. Who doesn't judge their neighbor, if only in secret?"

"Maybe," he said. "But that isn't killing. And when it comes to that . . . I'm not sure any of us has a right."

"You said they deserve to die!" I said. I tried to keep the beginnings of a smile off my face, but I probably failed.

"Yes," he nodded. "And so do I. Where does it stop?"

"So you're saying—"

He pointed at the Cadridians. "This isn't self-defense. If you want them dead, you'll have to kill them."

Kalla let out a long, low hiss. "This means nothing! He has admitted—"

Shapes exploded into being in the air around us, solid and shining, even in the morning light, with a radiance all their own. They were so real to me I felt sure that everyone must be seeing them, but none of the other mice showed any reaction.

"Kalla," I said. "You are a liar. There is one good mouse in Tira-Nor."

But Kalla was not listening. She turned in a tight circle, her mouth closed, her expression defiant.

"Colonel," I said, smiling. "Would you like to see something? Would you like to really see something?" I held out one paw.

He looked at my outstretched arm. "I don't understand."

"ElShua's army has returned."

He looked around at the gathered mice. Then his gaze flashed from me to KoTsu, who was still staring heavenward. Colonel Reese stood very still for a moment, and then slowly, as if to humor me, reached out and touched my paw.

Cold sparks flew from my fingertips to his. The fur on his head bristled and his eyes widened. He inhaled sharply, wobbled on all fours, and sank to his knees, his head pivoting slowly in all directions, his throat bobbing. "What are they?"

"The cold, flickering ones are the lost souls," I said. "The others, the ones who shine, are ElShua's army. They keep company with the Ghost Badger. Grayfeather is one of them, though he sometimes clothes himself in rags."

Reese's voice was soft, barely above a whisper. "When did they come?"

"They've always been here."

"We're doomed," he said.

I nodded. "But not all dooms are the same." I touched his forehead with my left paw and sucked the power back into my finger with a static tingle.

Colonel Reese blinked.

"Excuse me." I turned and plodded back down the slope to stand beside General KoTsu.

Queen IsaBel was watching from the mouth of the Royal Gate. She stood in shadow, except for the long swoop of her imperious nose. Her eyes glittered in the darkness like black jewels.

"What do you want, *brat*?" She bit off the last word as though it were a tough piece of rind clinging to an orange.

"I am here to make an offer," I said, hoping she would accept my terms. "How much is the safety of your people worth to you?"

"I should have killed you a long time ago." Her eyes scanned the Cadridians. She leaned into the sunlight and cupped one paw over her brow. "General KoTsu?" Puzzlement crept across her face.

KoTsu took a step toward her. "I am KoTsu."

The queen's eyes narrowed. She pointed at me. "Kill the brat," she said. "And then let us talk of peace."

I put one paw on his shoulder and leaned close to his ear. Cold fire crept from my fingers into his skin as I whispered, "See again!"

His eyes widened. His head moved from side to side, taking in the ranks of blind soldiers behind him, the queen, the palace guard, and Reese's militia—which was still forming into a ragged, undisciplined line on the slope above us. After a moment, his eyes found mine. "What shall you want me to do, Seer?"

"Answer the queen," I said.

KoTsu turned to the gate hole. "Queen IsaBel . . ." He gave me a questioning look over one shoulder, and I nodded for him to continue. "Does your previous offer still stand?"

Darkness flashed across her face. She smiled triumphantly. "It does!" she said. "Under the same terms."

I spoke so everyone could hear me. "And what would those terms be, General?"

KoTsu sniffed. "A queen's ransom," he said. "IsaBel, queen of Tira-Nor, has offered the mice of the Commons in exchange for her own life. We shall take any strong enough for the journey back to Cadrid."

Above us, a sound like creaking wood erupted from Reese's militia. Rage ignited their faces in a long line, as sudden and hot as a grass fire.

IsaBel's mouth clamped shut. Her eyes smoldered.

"Is that all?" I asked. "Just the mice of the Commons?" I emphasized the first word.

"In exchange for her comfort," KoTsu said, "IsaBel, Queen of Tira-Nor, has offered the kingsguard and palace servants. We shall take any strong enough for the journey back to Cadrid, and she shall keep two servants and her quarters in the Royal Palace."

Captain DeVree's expression did not change, but his back grew very stiff.

"And in exchange for her kingdom," KoTsu continued, "IsaBel, queen of Tira-Nor, has offered the lives of the lesser nobles. We shall take the strong back to Cadrid as slaves, and the weak shall remain here to pay taxes to support Her Majesty." KoTsu looked at me, then back at IsaBel. "Those were the terms."

For a long time no one spoke. But rage simmered beneath the surface. I suspect even the Cadridians felt something. Surprise, perhaps. Or shame.

In the silence, the fury gathered intensity. I said, "Now we know, Queen, how much the safety of your people is worth to you."

IsaBel stepped forward into full sunlight. Her face burned around piercing black eyes. She stabbed the air in my direction with one long finger and looked at Captain DeVree. "Kill him! Kill him now!"

DeVree stood motionless, his expression grim.

"Captain!" The queen shrieked. "Captain!"

I left KoTsu and approached Colonel Reese's militia. "Mice of Tira-Nor!" I called. "This moment brings you an opportunity. Before you, the army of Cadrid sent to destroy you stands helpless."

Silence. Mouse looked to mouse. Reese's militia stood too far up the slope to see the Cadridians clearly, but they sensed something was wrong.

Whispers cut through the silence. Helpless? Can it be true? What's wrong with them? Why do they stand so strangely?

"The mice of Cadrid are blind," I said. "ElShua took their eyes this morning, on the far side of the North Meadows. And I have brought them here to stand helpless before you."

"Kill them!" someone shouted. A weak cheer went up from the militia.

A cold current of air sloshed and swirled around me, barely visible, like a web of thin strands. *Dead and dead and dead and dead.*

Reese hushed them with a wave of one paw.

"Really?" I asked. "You would kill helpless mice? Mice ElShua has spared?"

"What would you have us do?" a voice from the back called.

"Feed them," I said. "Send them home with a blessing rather than a curse."

Silence. Every mouse considered this. Another mouse asked, "What's to stop them from coming back?"

"What's to stop them? You mean who. Who is to stop them from coming back?" I shook my head. "I believe they will stop themselves. And if not them, ElShua. Again. Are you afraid that the next time Cadrid brings an army to Tira-Nor, ElShua will be too busy to notice?"

Mice stared hard at the ground.

"But I do not think there will be a next time." I wheeled and held up both paws. "Mice of Cadrid," I said, "you came for honor, and you found it. You found justice as well as mercy. Believe me when I tell you that your master no longer wants Tira-Nor destroyed. Surrah Hammah's grudge against Tira-Nor has been forgiven. Your master is healed." I closed my eyes and imagined the mice of Cadrid waking and rubbing their eyes. In my mind, they looked around at the green fields of Tira-Nor and the blue skies above as if for the first time. "And so are you."

A breeze, warm as sunlight, tossed up like a ball from the North Meadows, kissed my face. Somewhere behind me footsteps thudded in a slow circle. I opened my eyes. At the edge of my vision I caught a flash of golden wings beating the air in arcs of pure white.

Kalla, too, stood near me, but her voice fell on my ears in undistinguishable syllables. I could not have understood what she said if I wanted to. Her voice sounded like a rusty hinge.

The mice of Cadrid huddled together, blinking into the sunlight.

Colonel Reese's militia approached KoTsu's army slowly, warily, but not defensively. Both groups relaxed. They joined in the center with no semblance of rank or order, and every visible sign of peace.

"Put me down!" IsaBel shrieked. "Down! Put me down! I will have your head for this, scum!"

Captain DeVree strode out of the Royal Gate with Queen IsaBel thrown over one shoulder. Her head hung down his back; her rear scraped the air. He looked from KoTsu to me to the massive group of mice on the meadow. The crowd hushed. DeVree stood before me for a moment as she beat her fists uselessly against his back. "We do not wish to pay the queen's ransom," he said, "so we will pay you the queen." He dumped her to the ground on her back.

She pressed one paw to her chest. Her mouth hung open. *How hard it must be to live in her skin,* I thought.

KoTsu looked from the queen to me. "But what shall I do with this queen?"

"Put her to work in the kitchens," I said.

Chapter Thirty-Five

The Curse of the Seer

With Ahaz dead and IsaBel gone, Tira-Nor needed a king. KoTsu's army marched over the northern horizon, and the mice of the Commons came to me for advice. Enough nobles were present to ratify my suggestion, so I told them, "I know of one good mouse in Tira-Nor." The following day I anointed Reese king of Tira-Nor and lord of the Known Lands.

Afterward, he gave me a tour of the palace, then begged to know what could be done for my comfort.

I told him I would like to have my old quarters back, the home stolen from my father.

"Is that all?" he asked. "But it's such a small thing, without any value."

◆ ◆ ◆

All of this happened many seasons ago, when I was young and the world draped itself in brighter colors.

There are advantages to being old. I say things now without worrying how they sound. Certain words come easily to my lips, though in my youth I couldn't speak them without feeling like an impostor. "Behold," I sometimes say now. And even, "forsooth."

The mice of Tira-Nor don't know how young I really am. They don't know these words sounded ancient when I was a kit, and so they pass me off as an old coot who has lost his mind, but who still carries a power to be feared, if not understood. Sometimes I pump my knees and turn circles in the Great Hall and say, "Come again later!" just to see the eyes of the kits go wide. But AlBaer's habits never wholly fit me; I am more comfortable in my own rhythms.

My eyesight grows dim now. I see the lost souls almost constantly, or I would if they dared show themselves. They seem to fear me, an old mouse of little strength. I marvel at this. Whenever one strays too close, I unleash my tongue. The power entrusted to me still flows as sharp as razor wire.

For many seasons I lived in our ancestral home, but it was a lonely place, full of regrets best left undisturbed. Recently, a young mouse of the kingsguard helped me move my things to RuHoff's cave. The mice of Tira-Nor consider the place haunted, and they are right. Memories swirl through my new home like ghosts.

But they are good ghosts. Sometimes when the moon shines through the low entrance I imagine soldiers standing there, keeping watch. Other times the place is as empty as a fool's promise, or the cap of an acorn. The world between grows brighter as the world of my old age dims.

Who can tell which is which when one's eyes are as bad as mine? Sometimes I complain to ElShua; a seer ought to be able to see.

In one corner of the ceiling, between the etchings of RuHoff and Glyn, I have added my own island in colors mixed from berries left on my doorstep. I wonder sometimes if anyone will notice it, if anyone will take the time to puzzle out the meaning of my words. Perhaps in their day Glyn and RuHoff wondered the same thing.

My contribution to the slab of ages carries none of RuHoff's wisdom, none of Glyn's wit. Yet somehow it exposes and mocks all of my swollen inadequacies. And, occasionally, it makes me laugh.

Judgment misses
Mercy's kisses.

No one comes to me any more, and I fear for the city when I am gone. How long can any people survive when every mouse wears a disguise? When truth is sold for a pittance?

Alas, darkness is surely coming. For Tira-Nor. For Cadrid.

For me.

I lie in the corner on my straw pallet and watch as RuHoff's etchings fade slowly away, and I wait for the darkness to consume me. I feel cold and warm at the same time, yet I am not afraid. The darkness I see is not a river. It is not empty.

Perhaps this is the final irony of my life. Now, at the end, I will see the darkness from which there is no escape, and I will not fear it.

It is a pleasant riddle.

The answer brings a smile.

Behold! The darkness isn't dark at all.

The End

Glossary

The Commons: The largest section of Tira-Nor. Home of the commoners who make up the city's majority. The Commons is the shallowest level of the city, the section closest to the surface. In recent years it expanded downward as the population of the city increased and the need for additional chambers grew more urgent.

ElShua: The soft-spoken Creator. The Maker of the universe and Ruler of all living things. The name literally means "who whispers," indicating that the Creator speaks quietly and with great significance. To a mouse, a whispered message is more important than a shouted one. But the greater implication of "who whispers" is that of nearness. Since a whisper cannot be heard from far off, ElShua must be close at hand. A more complete and accurate translation might be "He who is so close He need only whisper to be heard."

The Families: A section of Tira-Nor reserved for the upper class.

Gate: An entrance into, or exit from, Tira-Nor. A hole in the ground protected on the inside by a series of guard chambers and booby traps. The twelve gates of Tira-Nor are named for their locations around the city. Because Tira-Nor is a city of multiple layers, its gates vary in depth, size, and complexity.

Glowstone: A phosphorescent rock used by the mice of Tira-Nor to light the tunnels and chambers of their underground city.

The Great Owl: Death. To mice, he is an agent of ElShua, though one greatly feared. It is significant that mice see death as a nocturnal predator shrouded in mystery. The Great Owl comes in darkness, unseen and unheard. He is rarely anticipated. A vast number of conflicting myths and fables surround the Great Owl. Some mice, most notably the seers, claim that a literal spirit being—swooping on outstretched wings as white as snow—descends to bear the souls of the dead to eternity.

The kingsguard: The personal bodyguards of the king of Tira-Nor, and the elite fighting force of the city. Also, the section of Tira-Nor that houses the kingsguard warriors. This section of the city encompasses and connects all others, somewhat like the hub of a wheel. From the Kingsguard level of Tira-Nor, it is possible to get to any of the other sections.

Lord Wroth: The god of the rats, prairie dogs, weasels, and possums. Many mice believe Lord Wroth to be a real spirit being, while others say the power of the legend of Lord Wroth lies in the fact that the rats believe it. Rat theology describes a great number of different gods acting in various ways with different forms of life. Thus the rats worship Lord Wroth, the mice of Tira-Nor follow ElShua, the mice of Cadrid follow Kalla, the white mice of Leer and the serpents of the Known World serve SeeEqueq. Although the rats seem to comprehend the mouse ideal of a single Creator, they greatly resent it—possibly because they believe it to be true, but don't want it to be.

Militia: Volunteers and conscripts. Mice who are unaccustomed to the disciplined life of a soldier are, in times of dire need, taken into civilian military service to defend the city. The militia is usually commanded by two or three officers of the kingsguard.

SoSheth: The first king of Tira-Nor, anointed by TaMir many seasons before the events of this book. TaMir later revoked the blessing of ElShua he had previously given to SoSheth, and from that point on SoSheth never esteemed TaMir, nor the God TaMir claimed to serve. It was also at this point that So-Sheth began to act strangely, and many in his service noticed that he became volatile, short-tempered, and unpredictable.

TaMir: The seer who anointed SoSheth—and later JaRed—king over Tira-Nor. Marked from birth as a seer by his all-white fur, TaMir was dedicated to ElShua by his mother and trained under RuHoff.

Tira-Nor: Literally, "the city of promise." Generations earlier, according to stories handed down by the elders, ElShua drove the ancient prairie dogs from the city and gave it to the followers of the mouse TyMin, founder of Tira-Nor.

the Royal Palace
Royal
West
the Kingsguard
The Families
The Great Hall
Open
Common
Shade
Wind

TIRANOR
the
Tunnels
North
Mud
Seed
Tower
East (gate)
The Commons
N
T
Forest
denotes a gate

Tall Grass
Dry Gully
Round Top
To West
Exiter
White River
TyMin's Path

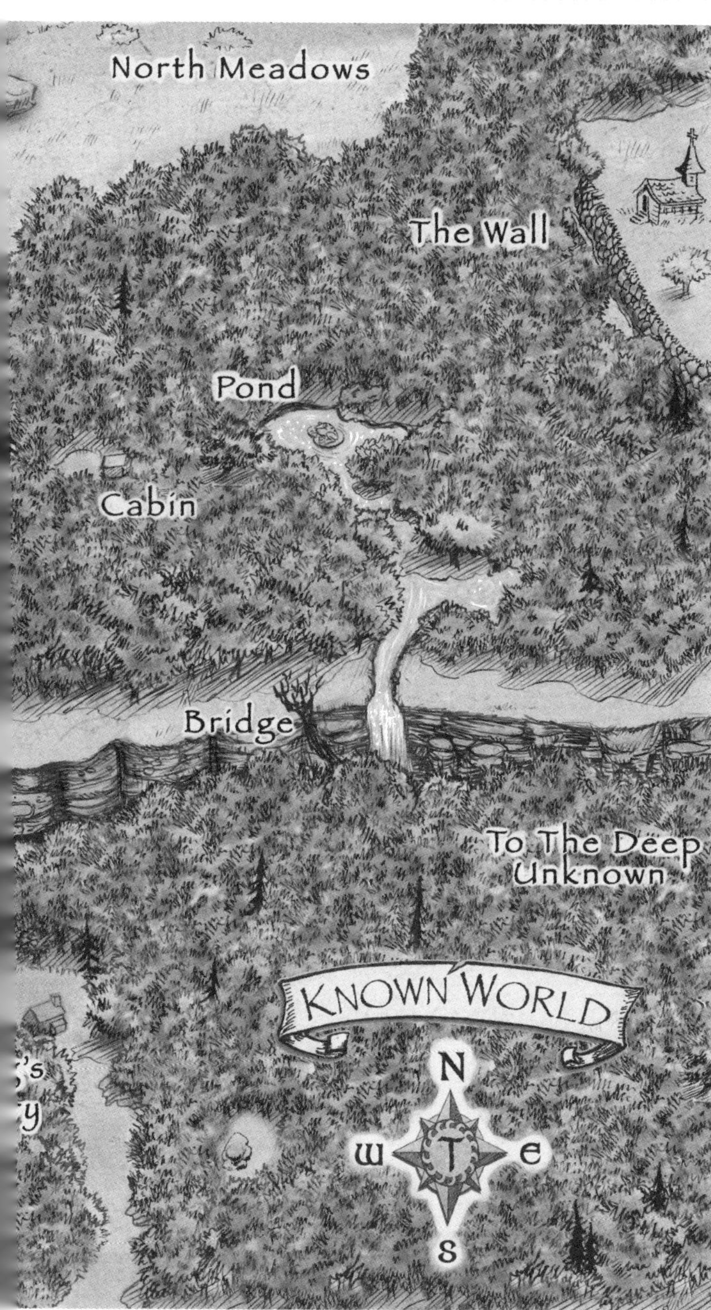
North Meadows
The Wall
Pond
Cabin
Bridge
To The Deep
Unknown
KNOWN WORLD
N
W
E
S

When you buy a book from **AMG Publishers**, **Living Ink Books**, or **God and Country Press**, you are helping to make disciples of Jesus Christ around the world.

How? AMG Publishers and its imprints are ministries of **AMG (*Advancing the Ministries of the Gospel*) International**, a non-denominational evangelical Christian mission organization ministering in over 30 countries around the world. Profits from the sale of AMG Publishers books are poured into the outreaches of AMG International.

AMG International Mission Statement

AMG exists to advance with compassion the command of Christ to evangelize and make disciples around the world through national workers and in partnership with like-minded Christians.

AMG International Vision Statement

We envision a day when everyone on earth will have at least one opportunity to hear and respond to a clear presentation of the Gospel of Jesus Christ and have the opportunity to grow as a disciple of Christ.

To learn more about AMG International and how you can pray for or financially support this ministry, please visit **www.amgmissions.org**